"Let's drive out to the beach," I said. "We can talk there."

Adam gave me an odd look but obediently turned the car in the direction of the beach. When we got there we parked, and I slipped out of my strappy sandals.

The moon was floating low over the water, and the surf roared like a distant train. With a little stab of surprise, I realized that in the past few weeks, I'd actually begun to like the beach. I knelt down and started digging in the sand with my fingers.

"Crikey, Mary Ann," said Adam. "Is this any time to be building sand castles? Are you going out of your flipping mind?"

"Look here," I said, burrowing my hand under the sand and firming the sand around it. "Maybe they're not digging a hole," I said. "Maybe they're digging a tunnel. They're tunneling into the castle!"

Dear Readers:

Thank you for your unflagging interest in First Love From Silhouette. Your many helpful letters have shown us that you have appreciated growing and stretching with us, and that you demand more from your reading than happy endings and conventional love stories. In the months to come we will make sure that our stories go on providing the variety you have come to expect from us. We think you will enjoy our unusual plot twists and unpredictable characters who will surprise and delight you without straying too far from the concerns that are very much part of all our daily lives.

We hope you will continue to share with us your ideas about how to keep our books your very First Loves. We depend on you to keep us on our toes!

Nancy Jackson
Senior Editor
FIRST LOVE FROM SILHOUETTE

A RISKY
BUSINESS
Janice Harrell

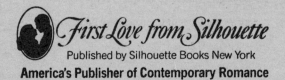

First Love from Silhouette

Published by Silhouette Books New York

America's Publisher of Contemporary Romance

SILHOUETTE BOOKS
300 E. 42nd St., New York, N.Y. 10017

Copyright © 1987 by Janice Harrell

ISBN: 0-373-06229-X

First Silhouette Books printing April 1987

America's Publisher of Contemporary Romance

Printed in the U.S.A.

RL 5.2, IL age 11 and up

JANICE HARRELL is the eldest of five children and spent her high school years in the small, central Florida town of Ocala. She earned her B.A. at Eckerd College and her M.A. and Ph.D. from the University of Florida. For a number of years she taught English at the college level. She now lives in North Carolina with her husband and their young daughter.

Chapter One

Dr. Mary Ann Taylor
Lieutenant Mary Ann Taylor
Captain Mary Ann Taylor
Sister Mary Ann Taylor
Mother Mary Ann Taylor

I laid down my pencil and looked at my list with a feeling of depression. I had reached the beginning of my junior year without a single boy paying the slightest attention to me. Obviously, a life of spinsterhood stretched before me. Unless I took drastic steps I was going to be Miss Mary Ann Taylor my whole life. I decided, however, that becoming

a nun was a bit *too* drastic a step. I drew a line
through "Sister Mary Ann Taylor" and "Mother
Mary Ann Taylor," and, sighing, stuffed the list
inside my geometry book. Everyone else had left
the classroom minutes ago when the final bell for
the day had rung. The building was almost deserted when I gathered my books and left.

I went outside, wincing as I hit the bright sun-
shine. To my right, school buses were slowly pulling out of the loading zone and cars stuffed with
kids were tearing out of the parking lot, tires
squealing. I turned in the opposite direction. I
wasn't in the mood for human company.

As I moved along the path past some floppy
cabbage palms, I noticed the dark head of Adam
Kincaid bent over a trowel. He was uprooting weeds
among the geraniums.

Adam was the youngest of the Kincaid brothers.
His next older brother, Mark, had graduated two
years before so I didn't really know him or the old-
est Kincaid boy, Steve, but I had heard about how
they had once managed to get a full-grown donkey
into the principal's office. By the time it had been
discovered the next morning, it had not only se-
verely damaged the office carpet, it had eaten several students' permanent records. Another of their
feats had been painting the town water tower with
the legends "Class of '83" and, later, "Class of
'84." The tower still said "Class of '84." Since the

Kincaid brothers had graduated, nobody had been crazy enough to try to bring it up to date.

So I wasn't surprised to see that Adam was working off detention hours by weeding the school geraniums. Detention hours were practically a Kincaid family tradition. In fact, when Mark graduated, some people said a plaque should be put in the garden in honor of all the time the Kincaids had spent there.

Adam looked up as I went by. "Mary Ann!" he called. Startled, I stopped suddenly and my books slipped out of my arms. I scrambled to pick them up, especially the geometry book and the incriminating slip of paper that had spilled out of it. When I straightened up, I saw that he was looking at me. "Would you go steady with me?" he asked.

I could feel hot color rising to my face.

"Kincaid!" came the booming voice of Mr. Furness, the assistant principal. "Get back to work. What do you think this is, a picnic?"

Adam muttered something under his breath, but bent over again swiftly. "Meet me at Tizzy's at four and we'll talk about it," he muttered, not looking up at me again. Mr. Furness was heading in our direction. I expected he was getting ready to say a few choice words about how he knew all about Kincaids and how Adam could forget about pulling any tricks on him.

I walked away quickly, feeling uncomfortable and confused. What had made Adam say such a weird thing to me? I hardly even knew him. And the confusing thing was I could have sworn he wasn't teasing.

By the time I got home, I knew I was going to keep the appointment at Tizzy's. Curiosity is what I'd have to call my major personality flaw. I wondered what could be going on. He had looked almost as if he were pleading with me.

At four when I walked in Tizzy's front door, it looked as if half the high school were there eating ice cream at the little round tables. I quickly spotted Adam sitting alone at a table in the back. He saw me come in and waved at me. I was relieved to see that he was alone.

My heart began to pound and I had the uncomfortable feeling that my curiosity was leading me in over my head. Adam Kincaid wasn't a bit like the other boys I knew, the ones who sometimes called me up to check on the homework assignments and who tended to have bony wrists and blow their noses a lot. Adam was the tanned, fit sort that could obviously run a mile without getting out of breath. It was utterly impossible to imagine him blowing his nose. And now that I thought about it, when he lowered those dark eyebrows of his, he looked a lot like those Wanted posters in the post office.

I reminded myself that it wasn't too late for me to turn around and leave. But if I left, my curiosity would never let me rest. I took a deep breath and began making my way through the tightly packed tables.

"Hey, stuck up!" Amy said. "Aren't you going to even say hello? Come sit with us."

I was startled to see that I had bumped into Amy and Lisa's table without even noticing them.

"Can't right now," I said. "Talk to you later." I squeezed past them. I could feel Amy's and Lisa's curious eyes following me as I went back to where Adam sat glowering. Luckily, back by the video machines we were too far away for them to eavesdrop. Amy and Lisa were old friends of mine. But if I were going to do something foolish, I preferred for them not to know about it.

Adam was busy shredding a napkin with his brown fingers. I pulled out a chair and sat down across from him. "Hi," I said.

He stopped shredding the napkin and looked me right in the eye. "I need a steady girlfriend," he said bluntly. "Not just any girlfriend. It's got to be somebody my mom and dad would like, somebody really straight."

"Maybe you'd better just explain the whole thing," I said uneasily. "I'm not sure I follow you."

A girl in a frilled apron appeared and Adam ordered a double banana split.

I ordered a hot fudge sundae. I had the feeling I was going to need it.

"It's simple," he said when she left. "You saw me out there working at school. Well, I've got detention for practically my whole life for bringing a gun to school."

My mouth dropped open. "You brought a gun to school?" I whispered. I had never shared a table with a criminal before.

The waitress reappeared in record time and plopped down the banana split and the hot fudge sundae, but I scarcely noticed her. I didn't even remember to take a bite.

"I was just going to shoot a few birds on the way home," he said impatiently, "but the way they carried on when they found it in my locker you'd have thought I was planning a full-scale massacre of the faculty. My parents hit the roof."

"I guess so," I said.

"I don't know if you remember my brothers," he said, lifting the cherry off the top of the scoop of chocolate.

"I've heard of them. What are they doing these days?" I half expected to hear they were serving time in Raiford.

"Steve's working for the Miami police department," Adam said. "Married a nice girl, settled down. Mark's in the army. He married a nice girl, too. Settled down."

I suddenly saw a glimmer of light. "You think your parents would like you to find a nice girl, too?" I asked.

"I think so. That's the idea. They've got this big theory now that a nice girl steadies a guy ."

"But..."

"Look, I wouldn't expect you to do it for nothing," he said. "I'd pay you. This is important to me. They're talking about sending me to military school." I noticed that underneath his admirable tan, he was growing a little pale. "You know what those places are like? Hell on earth, that's what they're like." He took another bite of ice cream and eyed me steadily. "Well, will you do it?"

"This is so sudden..." I said.

"I don't have time to play around. They've already sent off for the brochures of these fascist-type schools. How much do you want to do it for me?"

I imagined what my parents would think if they found out Adam was paying me to go out with him and involuntarily shuddered.

"You won't do it?" he asked, his brows lowering in disappointment.

"Well, I'm not sure I understand exactly what you have in mind," I said.

"A business arrangement, that's all," he said curtly.

"But we'd have to go out together, right?"

"Sure. But don't think I expect you to hang around with me all the time. We don't have to run this thing into the ground."

"No, of course not," I said. It sounded like an odd arrangement. But in spite of that, I had to admit it had certain attractions for me. Part of what got me down about never having any dates was the disgrace of it all. Like being picked last for volleyball in the fifth grade, it was humiliating. It occurred to me that what Adam was proposing could be the solution to my problem as well as his.

"Just the big dances, a date on the weekends. That ought to do it," he said.

Thinking of having an actual date on the weekend, I began to feel slightly faint. And then when I thought of the dazzling social prestige of actually going steady! Lisa and Amy would never believe it.

"You won't have to pay me," I said in an amazingly calm voice. "Just pick up the check for the times we go out together. That's enough."

"Are you serious?" he asked. "You'll do it?"

"Well, I don't see why it shouldn't work out. It's worth a try."

"You're a sport, Mary Ann," he said warmly. "A lot of girls wouldn't understand the fix I'm in. You know, the minute I thought of this plan I knew you'd be perfect for it."

"You did?"

"Yeah. I've always figured you had a lot on the ball. I knew you'd see what I was up against. And then you're so straight, you're just made for the part. Those little round collars, the neat, ordinary brown hair, nothing flashy, the good grades, the way you hang around with all those kids that go to church all the time. You're just the type my parents go for. You even sort of look like Steve's wife, Ernestine."

I looked down at my melting sundae and stuck a spoon in it. I had been right. I was going to need the morale boost a hot fudge sundae provides.

"And you aren't going with anybody either," Adam went on thoughtfully. "That was important. I had to get somebody that was completely unattached."

I held up a hand in the hope of stopping any more explanations on why he had chosen me. "That's okay, Adam," I said, smiling weakly. "I'm glad to help out. Don't worry about it."

"I tell you, sometimes I feel like wringing Mark's and Steve's necks for them," he said, his face darkening. "What a mess they left me in! Everybody keeps expecting me to pull all those crazy stunts they did. I'm not that kind of guy, but now that I've blown it taking that rifle to school, who's going to believe me?"

"I can see it's a problem," I said. I was already thinking of how I would break it to my friends that

Adam and I were going steady. I would have to be very careful the way I went about it. It wouldn't work for me to act as if this were some great love affair because it would be all too obvious that it wasn't. I had very little practice in deceit, being, as Adam had noticed, very straight, but I could see right away that the best approach would be to say as little as possible. That way I wouldn't risk tripping myself up.

"Here," he said. I looked up and was startled to see that he had taken off his class ring and was pushing it across the table to me.

"No!" I yelped.

He looked confused. "I thought you said . . ."

"Not yet," I whispered. "Don't you think we'd better go out together a couple of times before you give me the ring?"

He looked relieved. "Oh, I see what you mean. Okay." He slipped the ring back on his finger. "The only thing is, we'd better not waste any time. My parents mean business. Let's go to a movie tomorrow night."

"On a school night?"

"You don't go out on school nights?"

"Well, this *is* an emergency. And I can probably get my homework done before we leave."

"Pick you up at 7:30," he said. He pushed his chair out and started to get up.

"Wait a minute," I said, hastily swallowing a bite of ice cream. "We'd better leave together."

"Oh, yeah," he said. "I forgot."

I pushed the melting sundae away. "I don't have to finish this," I said. "We can go."

He smiled at me. "You really are a sport, Mary Ann. And I want you to know that I really appreciate this. I just hope I can do you a favor sometime."

As I got up I shook my hair out of the neat look Adam had so tactlessly commented on. I should be enjoying myself, right? In a very short while, I would actually be going steady.

Adam paid for both our ice creams at the cash register. Outside, when he opened his car door a breeze lifted his dark hair and I noticed it was too long, but with that perfect straight nose and the tan of the century, he was certainly better looking than any of the other boys I knew. He flashed me a grin and I somehow managed to smile back.

When I got in my own car I found myself craning my neck to get a glimpse of myself in my rearview mirror. Did I really seem as boring and uptight as Adam had hinted? The rearview mirror was uninformative. The same familiar hazel eyes that I had confronted every day of my life looked back at me except that they looked slightly out of focus. It is possible they were having a little trouble adjust-

ing to the idea of being Adam Kincaid's steady
girlfriend.

As I drove home, a stab of panic hit me, but I
told myself to keep calm. I should be able to handle this situation. The fact that I had reached sixteen without actually going out with a boy did not
necessarily mean that I was a hopeless human
being. I reminded myself that I was intelligent and
reasonably adaptable. I certainly could adjust to a
simple business arrangement that only required me
to pretend to be going steady. Nothing could be
easier, in fact. Right?

I hadn't been back at my house five minutes
when Amy showed up at the front door. I was startled to see her. She must have left her ice cream half
eaten in order to make it to my place so fast.

She plunged into the living room. "Tell me
everything," she said breathlessly. "Every detail.
Why didn't you tell me you were seeing Adam Kincaid?"

"Well..." I said. "Oh... I don't know."

"I hope you weren't afraid I'd try to steal him
from you? I'm not that kind of person. Besides,
Daddy would kill me if he found out I was dating
one of the Kincaid boys. What do your parents
think?"

"I'm not sure," I said.

"You're keeping it a secret?" she said, her eyes
widening. "Isn't that risky?"

"Not exactly a secret...."

"What's the matter with you, Mary Ann? You're not acting like yourself at all. I've never seen you shilly-shally like this." She looked at me as if she were about to put me on a microscope slide. It was not going to be easy to keep a secret from anyone as naturally nosy as Amy.

"Well..." I hedged.

"I know," she said, throwing herself down in an armchair. "Love changes people, doesn't it? Now that Adam's come into your life you feel suddenly unsteady, unsure of yourself, that's it, isn't it?"

I decided it was best to divert the questions from me to her. "Is that how you felt when Larry came into your life?" I suggested helpfully.

"Of course not," she said. "I'm never unsure of myself, thank goodness. But I've read about people feeling like that. It's perfectly normal, nothing to worry about."

"That's good," I said.

"What I really want to know," she said, leaning toward me, "is what was happening back at Tizzy's."

"We were just having a little ice cream together," I said.

"No, I mean with Adam's ring."

"The ring?"

"Look, Mary Ann, don't deny it. Lisa and I saw him take off his ring and hand it to you and you shook your head and then he looked all upset and put his ring back on."

"Do you usually carry binoculars with you to Tizzy's?" I asked.

"Well, we couldn't help but notice. I mean, naturally, it caught our attention because we didn't even know that you *knew* Adam very well and there the two of you were sitting together. But okay, if you don't want to tell me, don't. We've only been friends since the fifth grade and remember how I told you absolutely everything about when Larry started asking me out, even the dumb embarrassing things I said." She shot me a challenging look.

"The ring," I said, thinking fast. "Yes, the ring. Well, as you said, I've been feeling kind of unsure..."

"Not ready to make a commitment like that," she said.

"That's right."

"Not sure you feel he's that special to you," she said with bright-eyed interest.

"I just thought it was a little too soon, that's all," I said lamely. "I don't know..."

"You don't have to explain to me," she said. "I understand perfectly and you are so right. Why tie yourself down to one boy? The world is your oyster. He's not the only fish in the sea. You're too attractive a girl to tie yourself down to one guy."

"I am?" I said, startled, but Amy didn't seem to notice. She had gotten up and was pacing the floor.

"I see it all," she said. "It's that sweet, fresh-faced look of yours that drew him to you. Wild boys are always attracted to nice girls, don't you think? But have you thought of this? What will you say to your parents if he ends up in jail like his brothers?"

"His brothers aren't in jail," I said. "They've both got good jobs and families."

"They sure spent twenty-four hours in the slammer for painting the water tower that last time," she said.

"Oh, that. Well, that was just a prank."

"I think you're right," she said, looking at me warmly. "True love conquers all."

Just then the doorbell rang and I had to go answer it. By now, I was not surprised to see that it was Lisa.

"Amy!" she exclaimed. "I didn't know you were stopping off at Mary Ann's." She stepped inside and looked at Amy accusingly.

"I just happened to stop by," said Amy, avoiding her eyes.

"Well, what's the story?" asked Lisa. "Tell me. Tell me."

"He tried to give her his ring, but she wasn't sure she was ready to be tied down yet," said Amy.

"And I didn't even know that you knew Adam!" Lisa squealed. "Honestly!" She grabbed both my hands. "Tell me *all* about it. Don't leave out anything. Oh, I wish something romantic like that would happen to me. How did you ever keep it a secret? I just adore those tough-looking-type boys, don't you? Those eyes of his! And that tan is to die! You are so *lucky!*"

"True love conquers all," said Amy smugly. "She's not a bit worried about what her parents think of him."

"That's wonderful," breathed Lisa. "I wish something like this would happen to me someday."

I smiled weakly. The fact was I had begun to worry about what my parents were going to think.

Chapter Two

Adam Kincaid?" said Mom, looking up from her book. "Is he that nice boy who helped out with soup kitchen last month?"

There have been few times I've been glad my mother is an intellectual but this was one of them. It would not be fair to describe Mom as vague. She was just genuinely more interested in what Kierkegaard said about Being and Nothingness than in what the neighbors were saying about the Kincaid boys.

"I think you're thinking of Charlie Sadler, Mom. Adam is darker." And better looking, I added to myself. "We're going to a movie tonight," I said.

"On a school night, dear?" She frowned up at me.

"We won't be late getting in," I said. "And I've already done all my homework."

Another mother might have noticed that her daughter was about to go out on her very first real date ever. But just as Mother had scarcely seemed to notice my dateless state before ("There's plenty of time for all that later, dear. You're so young.") so she scarcely noticed this important milestone.

"Well, whatever you think," she said absently. "Your father is working late tonight, so maybe we'll just use up the last of that leg of lamb."

For the momentous occasion of my first date I chose my khaki-colored dress with the bright coral lining that showed at the collar and on the flip side of the sash. I decided on it for the simple reason that it was the most dashing thing I owned. Adam's remark about those little round collars of mine had hurt. I peered at myself anxiously in the mirror and tried to imagine what sort of girl Adam would be going out with if he hadn't had to pick somebody he thought his parents would like. I dimly remembered seeing him with a blonde at the beach a couple of months ago. She had a thick mane of blond hair that fell over into her eyes and was wearing a swimsuit that skated thinly along the lines of indecent exposure. Recalling that, I recklessly unbuttoned the front of my dress an extra button.

I heard the doorbell ring and jumped a mile. "A simple business arrangement," I reminded myself as I went to answer the door. Mother was already chatting with Adam when I got there. I decided I was going to have to be a little faster on my feet in the future.

She waved to us cheerfully as we left. "Have a good time, kids," she said.

"I like your mom," said Adam. "She doesn't look me up and down, all suspicious, the way a lot of other mothers do."

"It's because she doesn't gossip," I said as I got into the car. "She's never heard of your brothers."

"I wish there were more out there like her," he said feelingly, as he got behind the wheel.

A few seconds later we were driving along Indian River Drive heading toward the center of town. Adam cast a wistful glance at the palm trees leaning over the glassy surface of the intercoastal waterway that ran along the drive. "Great time to be out in a boat," he said. "Don't guess you like to fish."

"I've never tried it."

"You've never been fishing?" he asked in disbelief.

I found myself blushing.

"Sorry," he said. "I was just a little surprised there for a minute, that's all. The thing is, what I've been thinking is that this going steady business could take up a lot of time."

"It could cut into a fellow's fishing time all right."

"That's just what I've been thinking," he said. He smiled at me, showing perfect white teeth. "Want to learn to fish, Mary Ann?"

"Not much," I said. "You know, it's not too late to back out of this plan, if you think it'll take up too much of your time."

"No, no, I wasn't thinking about that. Heck, military school would be a hundred times worse."

Thanks a lot, I thought.

"I don't know if you realize it," he went on, turning left on Palmetto Street, "but as a rule they don't build those military schools anywhere near beaches."

"Imagine that," I said.

He looked amused. "I'll bet you'd like fishing if you tried it."

"I guess there is a very small chance of that," I admitted. I was determined to be fair-minded. Everybody knew that spinsters tended to be set in their ways. If I didn't want to fall into the spinster trap, I should try to be flexible and open to change. At the same time, I was sure I was going to hate fishing. I have kind of a thing about worms. They disgust me totally.

When we got to the theater, I was dismayed to see that emblazoned on the marquee was *Return of the Worm King*. I clutched Adam's arm. "Isn't there anything else playing?" I asked.

"Just a Disney movie at the Harmony. I figured you would have already seen *Lady and the Tramp*."

I had in fact seen it twice when I was seven and I was afraid in my present state of mind that all those scenes where Tramp leads Lady through the back alleys and she ends up getting thrown into the pokey would hit a little too close to home.

"I guess this one will be okay," I said, swallowing.

"There are some X-rated flicks at the drive-in," he suggested helpfully. "They don't usually ask for any ID."

"*Return of the Worm King* could actually turn out to be pretty interesting," I said.

As it turned out, I wasn't able to eat a bite of my popcorn. All those worms on the screen completely wiped out my appetite.

I was surprised at how sympathetic Adam was when he saw how green my face was afterward when we were driving home from the movie. "Look, Mary Ann," he said, "about when we go fishing. Would it help any if I bait your hook for you?"

"I'd like that," I said falsely.

He walked me up to the front door and said good-night with a friendly pat on the shoulder.

A breeze was sweeping in from the waterway. I took a few deep breaths of it in the hopes fresh air would steady my stomach. As I was fitting my key in the lock, I noticed that a moving truck had pulled up to the Peebleses' house across the street. Since we live in a fairly desirable neighborhood just off the water, Dr. Peebles had had no trouble at all renting his house when he had gotten a year's visiting professorship in Germany. I remembered he had said he had rented it to a man from Miami who had a teenaged daughter with the odd name of Verena. I supposed they were just moving in.

I peered around our ixoria bush to try to get a better look at what was going on across the street but I saw no signs of life. I had been kind of hoping the girl would be about my age. Our neighborhood was not exactly full of young people. Across the street from us, on big lots that went right down to matching docks on the waterway, were both Dr. Peebles's house and the much bigger house of Mr. Fuller, the city councilman. On our side of the street was the ranch-style house that belonged to Mr. Stuart, the truant officer, a couple of cement block houses belonging to ''snow birds,'' retired couples who were only in Florida for the winter, and our sprawling cedar-shingled bungalow with its screened front porch. There wasn't any uniformity in the architecture because zoning hadn't really come to Fort Moulton yet. We were a little too far north of Miami to rate being a glossy "planned community." Even though the town had grown a lot since my parents were kids, it still was in some ways like the overgrown fishing village it had been then.

Our neighborhood was a quiet one, where people liked to lie out in hammocks in the backyard when the mosquitoes weren't bad, and sit inside in the air-conditioning when they were. It was almost too quiet. No one even had a dog. Of course, I reminded myself as I went in, now that Adam had come into my life, it was possible that I already had enough excitement in my life even without having lively neighbors.

The next day in American History, for the first time I got a bit of an inkling about the sort of thing that moved Adam to make his desperate proposal to me. Adam had, of course, been in my American History class for weeks, ever since school had started but I hadn't paid much attention. I was too busy just getting adjusted myself to being at senior high. Because of crowded conditions at Spencer High, none of us got to move up to the high school until our junior year and then the shock was terrible—the crowds, the confusion of the high school, the strange new rules and regulations about one-way halls and one-way staircases and the weird lunch shifts. Everybody I knew was in sort of a zonked-out state of anxiety those first few weeks and it was only now, when I had a special reason to notice, that I realized Adam had an extra problem none of the rest of us had.

Mr. Jansen said, "We'll be discussing Jeffersonian principles and the downfall of Federalism. That means you'll need to have read pages 99 through 125 thoroughly—" he glared at some point behind me and growled "—and that means you, too, Kincaid. Just to be sure of that, I want you to be prepared to give a summary of Jefferson's principles to the class Friday." There was a chilling pause, then Mr. Jansen said, "Did you hear me, Mark?"

The next pause was even worse. I was shaking in my shoes and he wasn't even talking to me. "Kincaid, I said did you hear me," Mr. Jansen barked.

"Yes, sir," Adam said finally.

He didn't correct Mr. Jansen about calling him Mark. I suppose it would have just been pouring gas on the flames anyway. Mr. Jansen obviously didn't see any difference worth mentioning between Adam and his brother.

I looked over at Adam as we got up to leave class. His lips were pressed into a thin line and when he saw me at first he seemed to look right through me. Then his eyes cleared and he smiled. He got up and followed me into the hall. "I wonder what Mark did to Mr. Jansen," he said.

"I can't believe he called you Mark," I said. "I can see you really have a problem."

"Yup," he said. "You think they take guys my age in the French Foreign Legion?"

Hordes of kids thundered by us on all sides, rushing to the next class. "I better run," he said. "I can't be late to Mrs. Holloway's class. She's already got it in for me."

"Isn't there any teacher that doesn't have it in for you?" I asked.

He grinned. "Miss Blake. She's new this year." He took off at a trot. I lost sight of him for a minute but later I passed him at the up staircase. The teacher who was hall monitor was reading him the riot act about something. I moved on to chemistry with plenty to think about. If I had been getting the grief Adam was getting, I think military school would have started to look pretty good to me.

I saw Adam again at lunchtime. He spotted me and brought his tray over to sit next to me. "I've already mentioned to my mother that I've been seeing this really nice girl," he said.

"How did she take it?"

"Let's just say I could see the wheels start to turn in her mind," he said. "When do you think I can give you the ring? Nobody has got to know how long we've been going out."

Trays clattered around us and I was narrowly missed by a flying French fry but I paid no attention. Maybe Adam was right. There was no point in drawing all this out. "All right," I said. "But not here. Somehow I don't think this is the right atmosphere."

"Soon, though," he said. "I've got to get this show on the road."

"I understand your problem," I said. "Believe me, my eyes were opened in Mr. Jansen's class this morning. I see what you're up against."

He flashed me a grateful look.

"And *please* don't tell me again that I'm a sport, okay?"

"Right," he said. "You're not a sport. Whatever you say. Look, pizza tonight. I'll pick you up at six-thirty and I'll give you the ring then. Jeez, I hope this works."

I buttered my roll. "Don't worry. If you're shipped off to military school, I'll return the ring," I said.

"Don't even say it," he said. He began making short work of his cheeseburger, but a moment later I noticed his attention had wandered. Following his glance, I saw a new girl sitting alone at a table across the cafeteria.

In a school the size of Spencer, and when you've only been there a few weeks, it's hard to say for sure whether somebody is new or not. But this girl was new, all right. It wasn't just that she was sitting by herself, it was that girls who look like the Dragon Lady in the flesh are rare enough that I could be sure I had never seen this one before. She had black hair combed close to her head and so smooth it looked enameled. She used a blood-red lipstick that stood out against her white skin, she had a sweet-looking baby face and she was wearing expensive clothes. I personally thought she was the most sinister-looking creature I had ever seen. Adam was looking at her with fascination.

"Interesting-looking girl," I said. "I think she must be new."

He started. "Oh. Yeah. You can bet she's new. I'd have noticed her before now if she weren't."

I had been thinking exactly the same thing myself so I don't know why I should have been annoyed at his saying that.

He crumpled his empty milk carton in one hand and got up. "See you tonight," he said.

I sat there for a few moments staring meditatively at my cold mashed potatoes. All around me was the noise and confusion of hundreds of people talking, eating and dropping their silverware. I was beginning to have the feeling there were a few more pitfalls to this business of going steady than I had thought at first. It was going to be uncomfortable if I started feeling possessive about Adam. I got up and went to dump my trash into the garbage can at the front. Don't be silly, I told myself. You are not at all a possessive person.

Just the same, that afternoon when I got home from school, I was not happy to see the Dragon Lady girl carrying her books into the Peebleses' house across the street. On the driveway, a blond man in sunglasses was unloading a black leather couch from the truck onto a dolly. It was easy to imagine the Dragon Lady girl reclining on the couch in a satin robe while her sinister Chinese henchmen slunk around through the beaded curtains. If she were the type Adam went for, no wonder he thought I looked so conventional. And she was my new neighbor! How could I be so lucky. I had been wishing for somebody my own age to move in and now they had. That'll teach me to go around recklessly wishing, I thought, as I slammed the front door behind me.

Mother was closing *Being and Nothingness* with an absentminded smile on her face. I decided this might be a good time to mention that I was going out again tonight.

"Uh, I won't be in for supper tonight, Mom," I said. "I'm going out for pizza with a friend."

"With Amy?" asked Mom.

"Actually, it's Adam I'm going with," I said.

Mom wrinkled her brow. Now that she had finished *Being and Nothingness*, unfortunately, her powerful mind was left free to grapple with ordinary, everyday matters.

"That's the boy you went to the movies with last night, isn't it? You're going out with him two nights in a row? And on a school night?"

"Going out for pizza isn't exactly like going out, Mom. I have to eat anyway, right? It's not as if we're going to be out late."

She folded her hands and looked at me. "Adam seems to be a nice boy. Why don't you tell me about him?"

"Oh, just a boy," I said. "You know." I picked up my books. "I'd better go study. I've got an awful lot of reading for American History."

I holed up in my room with my books in order to get away from any further questions. I was afraid if she kept asking me things I might slip up and tell the truth.

At six Adam came to pick me up and we drove to Pizza Hut. We found a dimly lit booth there. A neon jukebox in the corner was playing some sad song I didn't recognize. A bored waitress slumped over to us, took our order and shuffled away.

"Have you made much progress into the downfall of Federalism?" Adam asked me.

"I'm about half finished," I said. "What about you?"

"Got it all sewed up. The spot I'm in, I can't afford to try to skate by," he said. "And actually, I'm kind of interested in Jefferson."

"You are?" I asked, startled.

"There you go," he said. "You're thinking I'm like Steve and Mark, aren't you?"

"Oh, no!" I said.

"I'm smarter than them. I make decent grades. I don't play practical jokes. I don't end up in jail."

"I guess it's hard to come along after a legend," I said.

"Tell me about it," he said bitterly. "All the time I was a kid, Mark and Steve were telling me lies, tying me up, dumping me in creeks, running off without me and now when they're finally away from home and I'm all by myself at last, it turns out it's like they'd never left. Heck, why am I telling you this junk? You're the one helping me out. Let's forget it." He rearranged the condiments on the table. "I see that new girl has moved in across the street from you," he said. "I saw her when I drove up this evening."

"Yes, they were still moving their things in this afternoon. They didn't seem to have much furniture," I said. "It wasn't a regular-sized moving van, just a medium-sized rented truck. I saw they have a black leather sofa."

"You watched them carrying the furniture inside?" he asked, shooting me an amused look.

"For a while. Curiosity," I admitted, "is a sort of major failing of mine. They've rented the house from the Peebleses for the year. The girl's name is Verena."

"Oh?" he said, putting on an unconvincing display of lack of interest.

He took off his ring and handed it to me. "Here you go," he said. "It's a lot too big for you. You've got such little fingers. You better wear it on a chain. And don't lose it, okay?"

I was afraid I would get all choked up with the romance of the moment.

Chapter Three

His ring!" said Lisa, awed. "You decided to go steady after all!"

"Oh, well," I said, fingering the ring on the chain. "Yes, I decided to go ahead. It's not as if I'm really interested in going out with anybody else."

"He cares for you more than you care for him, that's it, isn't it, Mary Ann." She sighed sentimentally.

"I wouldn't say that," I said. I twisted the ring until I suddenly remembered I might snap the chain.

"I remember how he begged you to go steady with him," Lisa said.

"Not exactly 'begged,'" I said.

"Love can be so sad and cruel," said Lisa. "Oh, I wonder if anything romantic will ever happen to me! Here I am sixteen years old and nothing, zippo, zilch romantic has ever come my way." She looked at me with moist eyes. "Tell me, what does it *feel* like to be having your very own romance?"

"Uh, nice," I said.

Lisa threw herself on my bed. "Honestly, sometimes I wonder if there's any hope for me at all. Now Amy's got Larry and you've got Adam. I'm probably positively the only girl in the junior class that's been left on the shelf. You can't imagine how that makes me feel."

"I have some idea," I said.

"What do you think it was that attracted Adam to you?" she asked.

"Gee, I don't know."

"That indefinable something," she said lyrically. "The *je ne sais quoi*, the who-knows-what that is bigger than both of you."

I interrupted her. "Lisa, tell me something. Do you think I look kind of boring and uptight?"

"Golly, no. What gives you an idea like that?"

"I think I struck Adam that way."

She was looking at me with wide, curious eyes.

"When he first met me," I added hastily.

"It just goes to show how wrong first impressions are, doesn't it. Here you turned out to be the one he really likes best of all! And you're not a bit like that girl I saw him with last summer, the one that wore the little bikini everywhere."

"What was she like?" I asked.

"I think she was just here for the summer. But I heard that at Buck Hawley's big party she got up and danced on the tables."

Lisa evidently noticed that this news did nothing to cheer me up because she leaned over and patted me consolingly. "But you don't have to worry about her, Mary Ann. They probably only went out together a couple of times. *You're* the one he asked to go steady. He's never gone steady with anybody before."

I managed a weak smile.

"I'd better be getting home," said Lisa. "It's getting close to suppertime."

I walked her to the door and watched her back out of our driveway. As she left, I noticed that a wizened little man in a striped T-shirt was carrying a suitcase up to Councilman Fuller's house.

While I was standing there watching him, the new neighbors' blue Buick pulled into their drive. Verena and a blond man wearing sunglasses got out of the car. The blond man said something to Verena and I saw her dart a glance at the man in the T-shirt. Then they both quickly averted their faces and hurried in the house.

"Dinner, Mary Ann," called Mom.

I went inside lost in thought. Had it been my imagination, or were Verena and her father trying to avoid being seen by that weird little man? I realized that I would love to believe there was something suspicious about Verena.

Dad was already busy slicing the roast when I got to the table. He looked up when I came in. "Your mother tells me you've been going out with a nice boy."

"Adam Kincaid," I said. I was glad I had tucked the ring well inside my shirt. I wasn't ready to explain that ring yet.

"I wonder if that's Stephen Kincaid's son," Dad said, laying some slices down on the platter. "He handles the insurance on our building. What's this boy like?"

"He's interested in Thomas Jefferson," I said. "He likes to fish."

"Speaking of fishing," Dad said, "that reminds me. I had lunch with Bill Thompson the other day and he told me they've sold the boat."

"I can't believe it," said Mom, serving herself some green beans. "All he ever talked about was that boat."

"Since the twins came, he said they never get out in it anymore so they decided to sell and put the

money away for the kids' education. But get this—
the guy who bought it paid for it with a suitcase full
of money."

"Imagine!" said Mom, her fork poising mid-
way. "Whatever did Bill say?"

"What could he say? That he wouldn't accept
cash?"

"I think that's disgusting," I said. "It's obvious
the creep is going to use the boat for running drugs.
You'd think they could put a stop to that kind of
thing."

"There's the little matter of evidence," said Dad.
"There's no law against buying a boat."

"They ought to patrol the coast and catch them
in the act," I said.

"Not too easy," said Dad. "With all the inlets,
the canals and rivers—even if the entire navy pa-
trolled it I'm not sure it would keep them from getting through. The coastline is like a sieve."

"I saw somebody with a suitcase over at the
Fullers' just a while ago," I said.

"Well, I hardly think it was full of money,"
Mom said. "Maybe the Fullers are borrowing a
suitcase from a friend or something. They're going
to the Keys for a few weeks any day now. Louella
asked me to turn on the lawn sprinkler for her if it
stays dry."

"I wish I had a few suitcases full of cash," said
Dad. "Now that we're shelling out for Phil's col-

lege, we're going to have to watch those pennies. Let's try turning off the lights when we go out of the room, okay? Is that too much to ask? And we could eat leftovers more often, too. What this family throws away would feed a Chinese family for a week."

"It's hard to get used to cooking smaller amounts now that Phil is away," said Mom guiltily.

"A penny here, a penny there, it'll all add up if we just keep an eye on what we're spending," said Dad.

I was disappointed no one thought the man with the suitcase seemed suspicious. Of course, they hadn't seen how unsavory the fellow looked or maybe they'd have looked at it differently.

The phone rang and I got up to answer it. "Hello?"

"Hey, Mary Ann? Adam."

"Oh, just a minute, Adam." I covered the receiver with my hand and said to Mom and Dad, "I want to take this call in my room. Could you just hang up for me when I get to the other line?"

I had gotten a lot of practice in deceit the past couple of days, but I didn't think I had better risk the challenge of talking to Adam about our arrangement with Mom and Dad listening to every word.

In my room, I waited until I heard the satisfying click of the living-room extension hanging up before I said anything. "Hey, Adam?" I said then. "I'm back now. I thought I'd better go to my room to talk," I said.

"Good idea," he said. "I'm calling from a pay phone myself. I just wanted to let you know that I told my parents about us going steady and they lit up like a chandelier. They can't wait to meet you. It turns out my dad knows your dad and he's heard all about what a fine, upstanding kid you are."

I was surprised to hear that Dad had been telling his insurance broker what a fine kid I was. I was used to having Dad bring home stories about how this person's daughter had made straight A's and that person's daughter spent all her spare time working with retarded kids and another person's daughter made all her own clothes, but I had gotten the distinct impression that when other people were bragging about their kids my father was sitting mutely by with nothing to contribute.

"This could be a problem," I said. "The thing is, I haven't told my parents yet. What if your dad spills the news to mine and they want to know why I haven't told them we're going steady?"

"So tell them."

"But they know we've only been out together twice!" I said. "It would seem strange."

"How can they know we've only been out twice? They can't keep track of every single thing you do. Just act as if we've been seeing each other for a while. That's what I did."

Adam seemed to have the strange idea that my parents took only a casual idea of where I was and what I did. That might be the way the Kincaid boys were raised, which would explain a lot, if true, but it certainly wasn't the way things were in our house. Mom expected to know where I was and what I was doing all the time.

"I could never pull it off," I said.

"It probably doesn't matter," he said. "I'll bet your dad and mine don't see that much of each other. Why get all worked up about it?"

I should have realized then that somebody who could bring a rifle to school and leave it in his locker without a care in the world was not the sort of person who tended to see trouble looming ahead.

"We ought to go out this weekend," said Adam. "Want to do some fishing?"

I was not sure I was ready to face worms again. I still hadn't completely recovered from *Return of the Worm King*.

"Why don't we go to church group instead?" I suggested.

There was a horrified silence. Finally, Adam said, "Church group?"

"Lots of kids go to church group Sunday night. It's not so bad. We have supper together and then they show a film or something and we talk about it. You have to admit your parents would like it," I said.

"Okay. I guess it won't kill me. Maybe afterward we could go frogging."

"Frogging?" I said suspiciously. "Is that something else that you do with worms?"

"Nah. You go out to Bowie's Creek with a flashlight. The flashlight stuns 'em. Then you spear them. Frog legs are really good eating."

I would have liked to think he was making it all up, but what he said stirred dim memories of my having noticed bunches of cars with lights being parked near the bridge by Bowie's Creek at night.

"I think I'd better come right home after church group," I·said. "School's the next morning, after all. I don't want to be out too late."

The funny thing was that back in the days before I met Adam I had somehow imagined that going steady would involve dances, moonlit nights and flowers.

Chapter Four

Mrs. Greenfield was full of ideas. She had taken a summer course in how to teach creative writing. If I had known that, I might have tried to get switched to somebody else's English class. The week before she had had us all bring shaving cream to class. We were supposed to squirt it on our palms and then describe it fully—the sight, smell, feel and taste of shaving cream. It looked, smelled and felt okay, but, as I could have guessed, it tasted terrible. Now Thursday, creative writing day, had rolled around again. I wondered what new treat was in store for us.

"Class," said Mrs. Greenfield brightly, her curly hair standing out like a halo around her head, "to day you will be writing an interview with one of your classmates. I'm sure you've all read profiles of famous people in the newspapers and magazines. This is your chance to find out if someone sitting next to you isn't just as fascinating in his own way as Richard Gere or Kathleen Turner."

I sneaked a look at Benny Gray, who was sitting beside me, four foot ten, freckled ear to ear and weighing in at two hundred pounds he was *not* as fascinating as Richard Gere.

"Find out about whomever you are interviewing," she chirped. "Notice looks, mannerisms. By use of sensory images, make your reader feel he can see the subject. Remember what we learned in last week's lesson with the shaving cream. I expect three hundred to five hundred words handed in at the beginning of class next Thursday. You will have today's class in which to begin your interview. Now starting with Tracy, please count off in twos."

The class began sounding off "one, two, one, two." I sighed with relief to see Benny paired with Mike Crichton. "One," I said, and turned to see who was sitting behind me. "Two," said Verena softly.

Oh, no! I got to interview Verena the Dragon Lady. It was even worse than tasting shaving cream.

"You don't have much time," said Mrs. Greenfield, "so make your questions to the point. Remember your profile should be as vivid as possible.''

I reluctantly scooted my desk around so that I was facing Verena, picked up my ballpoint and looked at her. "Tell me about yourself," I said flatly.

She smiled a little catlike smile. The corners of her mouth turned upward a little but there was no change in the rest of her face. She had a small, short nose and I noticed she had drawn a line above her lashes to emphasize the slightly almond shape of her dark eyes.

"Why don't we start with you?" she said sweetly.

There was a cacophony of squeaking of metal desk legs being dragged across the asphalt tile and a hubbub of confused voices around us while Verena and I eyed each other suspiciously.

"What do you want to know?" I said finally.

"You live across the street from me, don't you?"

"I think so," I said. "You've rented the Peebleses' house, haven't you?"

"That's right." We looked at each other in silence awhile longer. I reflected that at this rate it was going to be extremely hard to get three hundred to five hundred words out of this interview. The same thought had evidently struck Verena. She looked down at the blank sheet of paper before her and then said, "Why don't we just start with vital statistics. We can do the description from that. I'm five foot two, 98 pounds. I wear a size six shoe. What about you?"

I could just imagine the sort of dazzling, witty description that would result from my telling Verena's shoe size. "I think it would be better to talk about our interests," I said. "What are your hobbies?"

"I'm interested in clothes and the cinema and faraway places," she said. "What are *your* hobbies?"

"Needlepoint, reading mystery stories, working crossword puzzles and playing Scrabble," I said promptly. "I can get the answer to any word jumble in less than thirty seconds." I looked down at my blank paper. "I don't think hobbies are much help. There aren't a lot of words there. Maybe we should talk about our families next."

"I think we should just limit this to talking about ourselves," she said primly.

"If you say so," I sighed. We were rapidly running out of things to talk about. "Well, I guess we could talk about what we believe in. You know, our ideals and all that."

"You mean, what we think is important? I think a sense of style is important," she said.

I wondered if this was intended to be a comment on my plain jeans and shirt.

"I'm one of those people who's got to have beautiful things," she went on. "It's something inside me, a thirst, a hunger. I'm not like other people. I just cannot stand ugliness." She smiled serenely as if waiting for me to pat her on the head.

"I see," I said. I jotted down on my paper, "Subject is superficial, self-centered."

She gave a little laugh. "Life is so much easier for people like you," she said. "Ordinary people. I'm more like a delicate flower, an orchid. I need things that ordinary people don't need."

"Needs punch in the nose," I wrote.

"I need beautiful clothes," she went on lyrically, "a fine car, antiques, jewels, foreign travel. I can't help it. That's just who I am. I'm not cut out for the humdrum everyday world of work and school." She shot a swift contemptuous look at the kids around us.

"Uh, how do you plan to get all these things you need without working?" I asked.

"There are always opportunities for people with imagination," she said loftily. "People willing to take chances. Naturally, anything worthwhile takes effort. I just mean I don't intend to get stuck in some silly nine to five job. I want more out of life than that." She picked up her pen. "What about you? What did you say your name was? Mary Ann? It sort of fits you, doesn't it? Can I say you have the usual school activities?" She looked up. "I know what!" she said. "I can call it 'Just an Average Teenager.' What do you think?"

"A snappy title," I said.

"Writing essays is easy for me," she said. "I have an IQ of a hundred and thirty-five."

"How nice for you!" I said. I closed my notebook. Verena was the creepiest little twerp I had ever met. I figured a variation on the theme of despicableness was good for five hundred words. Piece of cake. I'd write it up over the weekend.

After this eye-opening interview I really would have preferred to avoid Verena, but everywhere I turned I seemed to run into her.

When Mrs. Lennon sent me to the office to pick up some handout sheets the next day, there was Verena, already standing at the counter. She was wearing a sultry wraparound dress splashed with large red poppies, a vivid foil to the glossy black of her hair. "I don't understand it," she was telling one of the secretaries in her soft voice. "There must be some foul-up somewhere."

"You do spell your name V-e-r-e-n-a C-h-a-r-l-e-s, don't you?" asked the secretary. "Coral Gables says they don't have your records. No record of you attending there at all."

"That's impossible. There must be some problem with their computer," said Verena. "Maybe it got filed backward. Maybe they listed me as Charles Verena. You'd be surprised how often that happens."

"Well, we could run it through that way and see what happens," said the secretary. "But the way they're dragging their feet it could be Christmas before we hear from them again."

"You really think it'll take that long?" said Verena, seeming almost cheered by the news.

"Well, almost, anyway," said the secretary. "Maybe you'd better get your folks to call them. We had one mother that had to go down there in person and get them."

"Oh, I don't mind waiting. They'll get it straightened out sooner or later," said Verena.

"Just remember that you're going to have to have the records eventually in order to graduate," warned the secretary.

"I'm not worried about that," she said.

After she turned away from the counter I moved up to it myself and asked for Mrs. Lennon's mimeographed sheets. I could not resist casting a curious look at Verena as she left. She had sort of an immature look, with her baby face, but she took the foul-up of her records with the kind of queenly calm I associated with older women. Most people would have blanched at the news that their old high school said they didn't exist. I could imagine myself in the same circumstances wailing, "What do you *mean* they say they don't have my records?" It would have been a case of "Call the police, call the National Guard! They can't do this to me!" But the news hadn't seemed to bother Verena at all. Maybe this was another example of how she was "special."

When the mimeographed sheets were plopped on the counter, I hoisted them and headed back to class, thinking, "It's a nerd! It's a pain! It's Verena! Girl of steel!" I returned to class smiling. Verena was the sort of girl it was a positive pleasure to dislike.

That afternoon when I got in from school, I noticed that our neighborhood was no longer quiet. Some loud music was coming from Verena's house.

I went in and dumped my books on the dining room table. Mom had closed all our windows and turned on the air-conditioning as a defense against the music. "Don't you feel like calling them up and telling them to turn it down some?" I asked her. "All that noise!"

"It's a little bothersome," Mom said. "But I hate to get on bad terms with the neighbors. Sweetheart, sit down. There's something I want to talk to you about."

I sat down, trying hard to look as if I had no guilty secrets.

Mom sat down at the kitchen table across from me. "You know this boy, Adam," she said.

I nodded mutely. I had suddenly remembered that I had a guilty secret.

"Well, Mr. Kincaid, Adam's father, was in your dad's office today and he happened to mention that you and Adam were going steady. How do you think he got that idea?"

"Dad didn't say we *weren't* going steady, did he?" I asked, looking at her anxiously.

"Your father didn't say much of anything. He was a little floored, I think, and naturally he wanted to talk to you about what was going on."

"You see, Adam and I *are* kind of going steady."

"But you have just been out with him a few times! Why it was only a week or so ago that you were going around here wailing that you never had any dates."

"Well...yes. But that was before Adam and I started seeing each other. And then, you know, things happened so fast..." I knew at once by the look on Mom's face that I had said the wrong thing. Mom and Dad were the sort of parents who believed that romances, particularly young people's romances, should move with the slowness of glaciers in the ice age.

"I cannot think it's wise to tie yourself down to one boy when you are only just getting to know him," Mom said.

"Mom, be real! Do you think battalions of boys are just waiting for me to break up with Adam so they can ask me out? They are not!"

"Well, sweetheart, you'll never know, will you, if everyone thinks you're going steady."

I took a deep breath. "It's not the way you think. It doesn't mean anything. So he gives me his ring? If either of us got interested in somebody else we would break up in a minute."

"He gave you his *ring*?" she said, looking anxiously at my fingers. Too late I realized that to Mom, rings meant engagement, marriage.

"I wear it around my neck," I explained. "It's just a little, uh, friendly token, that's all."

Mom looked at me closely. "Of course, we trust you implicitly," she said.

I tried to look trustworthy.

"You've always been *most* responsible," said Mom. "And your father and I have no wish to pry too much into your life. I can understand that times change and that you may not feel we understand the customs of your friends and maybe you're right. I do remember that your grandmother used to get upset about things that seemed ridiculous to me. I'm trying to keep that in mind. Just promise me that you won't feel tied to Adam. He's a nice boy, but you'll want to get to know all sorts of boys before you settle down with one."

"Oh, absolutely," I said, smiling brightly. I did not feel as if I were deceiving Mom. I had said there was no big romance between Adam and me and that was true. I thought it best if she and Dad remained ignorant of a few little details, however, such as my being in league with Adam to deceive his parents.

"I didn't realize Dad knew Adam's father that well," I said casually, as I got up from the table. "Do they see each other very often?"

"I don't really know, sweetheart. Why do you ask?"

"Oh, no reason. I just didn't realize they knew each other, that's all."

What had occurred to me, in fact, was that there were certain perils involved in letting my parents think that Adam's ring meant nothing at all while Adam's parents were being given the line that it was the next best thing to being engaged.

Sunday night, Adam picked me up to drive to EYC, our church's youth group. I was so glad not to be going fishing that I hadn't worried about anything else, but when we walked into the church hall together, I was conscious of a certain silence descending when everyone looked at us. It only lasted a moment, but I was left with the uncomfortable feeling that I had brought a tiger to dinner. It occurred to me suddenly that the kids at EYC probably figured Adam was some sort of ferocious criminal type because they could see him out doing detention every afternoon.

It did not help any that Adam suddenly glowered at Matt, the minister's son, when we came in.

Matt, a thin sensitive boy, visibly cowered. I wished I could have explained that there was nothing personal in the look Adam gave him. He was just looking that way because he wished he were somewhere else. As a matter of fact, I was beginning to agree with him.

"Oh, hot dogs and beans!" I said brightly. "I love hot dogs."

A space of several feet seemed to clear automatically around us as we stepped up to serve ourselves. Susan Finkernagle looked at us incredulously as Adam served himself four hot dogs. Personally, I had eaten lunch with him often enough not to be surprised at his appetite. He burned up a lot of calories in outdoor activities like doing detention.

Adam and I sat down, balancing our plates on our knees and I smiled at him uneasily. For some minutes, the only sound that could be heard was the sound of chewing, then all at once everyone around us started to talk frantically.

Adam leaned over, put his arm around me, and growled softly in my ear, "Mary Ann, you owe me for this."

I had the uncomfortable feeling the other kids were staring at us and I could feel myself growing hot. I should have realized that Adam and the kids at church group were not a good mix. I now saw that this was going to be a very long evening. Adam at church group? I must have been crazy. I promised myself that in the future I would avoid taking him out of his natural environment, whatever that was.

Chapter Five

Wednesday afternoon, the police threw up a roadblock a half a mile from Spencer High. They were stopping everybody. I pulled up behind a line of six cars. It was a manhunt, I told myself in excitement. A dragnet. They were looking for some desperate criminal. I wondered if it could have something to do with the wizened little man and the suitcase full of money. I was sure it did.

Glancing in my rearview mirror, I saw Verena's little blue Corvette approaching. Then she disappeared from my mirror. I turned around to look behind me and saw that she had pulled into a filling station. Then she turned her car around and headed back the way she came. I narrowed my eyes. Of course, it was possible she had left something at school and had gone back for it, but my mind was so full of sinister Chinese characters, wizened little men, drug-running boats and suitcases full of money I never considered that possibility for a minute. I was convinced she had some good reason for not wanting to be stopped by the police.

The police were so *dumb*, I thought. They should have put the roadblock where there was no room for people to turn around and escape.

Another of the cars ahead of me moved off and then another until it was my turn and I found myself looking out my car window at a state trooper wearing a peaked hat and wraparound sunglasses. With his red face and his massive bulk, he looked very intimidating. I even felt a momentary twinge of sympathy for Verena's attempt to escape the roadblock. When I took out my license and held it out to him, I wanted to tell him about the way Verena had escaped from the roadblock, but my mouth opened and closed like a fish's with no sound coming out. Finally, I managed to squeak, "Sir..."

He didn't seem to hear me. "Thank you for wearing your seat belt," he said heavily. "Here is your complimentary certificate for a free hamburger at Beatty's Hamburgers."

I looked incredulously at the certificate he handed me, which had a picture of a large hamburger on it and a slogan stamped across it saying "Safety Is Everybody's Business." No wonder the police hadn't bothered about where they put up the roadblock! They were only giving out hamburger coupons. This roadblock was no manhunt. How disgusting!

The trooper waved me on with one hand. He was already turning his steely gaze at the car behind me. I put my foot on the accelerator and moved my car slowly forward. Phooey. Of course, I was all in favor of people wearing seat belts, I thought, but I had got myself all set for something a little more exciting.

I drove home in a state of gloom. I couldn't stop thinking about Verena. I turned the car into our driveway and I looked over next door. There was still no sign of her car. Why hadn't she wanted to show her license to the police? I would have loved to know.

The next day at lunch Adam asked me, "Have you gotten to know that new girl, Verena, yet?" He bit into his hamburger.

"A little," I said. "I had to do a profile on her for English class."

"With you two living practically next door to each other, I guess you'll be getting kind of chummy."

I thought it more diplomatic not to comment on that possibility. Verena was sitting not far from us, talking to Billy Menlo. She was wearing a wrap-around dress of white eyelet material that showed a long expanse of leg where it opened at the side. Adam seemed to be having some difficulty taking his eyes off of her.

I cleared my throat. "I haven't heard Mr. Jansen yelling at you the last few days," I said. "Do you think that's a good sign?"

"Yeah, since I made a hundred on the unit test he's starting to notice that I'm a little different from Mark," Adam said, turning his attention toward me with an effort. "The longer I go without getting into trouble the better, of course. This business of me going around with you helps. You know Mr. Bowers, the chemistry teacher?"

I nodded. "Well, after class yesterday, he told me he had noticed that we were going around together and you know what he said? He said if he were doing the picking, you were just the girl he would have picked himself."

It was nice to know that at least I was capable of attracting a bald, potbellied middle-aged chemist who already had a wife and five children, even if I was having some difficulty keeping Adam's attention.

"I was surprised," he said. "I mean, who'd expect the teachers to notice we were going around together? But it's good. Some of that respectability of yours is bound to rub off on me."

"Or it could go the other way. Some of your rotten reputation could rub off on me."

"Aw, get out of here," he said. "Nobody'd ever think you were up to anything. You're just not the type, Mary Ann."

I was not sure this was a compliment.

"Let's face it," he said. "Your average girl is innocent unless proven guilty. With me, it's just the other way. Like if a cop comes on a couple of guys walking down a dark alley chances are he asks them what they're up to, wants to see their ID, maybe frisks them. You know what he'd do if he found a couple of girls walking down a dark alley? Tell them it wasn't safe and give them a ride home. Let me tell you, there's no justice."

"When I think about how women still don't get equal pay for equal work, I guess I have to agree with that," I said.

"Don't start giving me that women's lib stuff. Look, I'm all for equal pay for equal work so don't go looking at me that way. You think I'm some kind of Neanderthal man or something? But you can't deny boys and girls are just different."

"Yes, I've noticed that."

His eyes drifted over to Verena, who was batting her mascaraed lashes at Billy. "Like, girls are more decorative," Adam went on. "You might even say that girls *ought* to be decorative. Looking good is an important part of being a girl."

"I think that's the most ridiculous thing I've ever heard," I said sweetly. "Look, Adam, if you want a better view of Verena, why don't you just go over and ask if you can join them."

"Verena?" he said, flushing a little. "Was I looking at her?"

"Verena is *so* interested in looking good," I said. "In fact, clothes are practically the chief thing she cares about. I found that out when I interviewed her. Maybe the two of you could get together and talk about how important it is for girls to look good."

I gathered my things together on my tray and got up to leave.

"Hey, you aren't mad are you?" said Adam, his brows lowering as he got up.

"Certainly not," I said, walking up to the trash cans. After I cleared my tray, I tossed it onto the stack of trays where it made a nice angry clacking sound.

"Okay, well, I'm glad you're not mad because I thought maybe you'd like to go out to the beach this afternoon. We could go to Jack Island. I'll show you how to track animals."

"You're not going to shoot anything, are you?" I said suspiciously.

"Heck no. Nobody can shoot on Jack Island. It's a game preserve."

We walked outside while I avoided Adam's eyes by looking at the ground. "You know, I don't think we have to go out together every single week," I said.

"Well, if you don't want to...." He scowled.

"No, I mean, if *you* don't want to...." I said.

"Heck, *I* want to. I just asked you, didn't I? Look, Mary Ann, what are you getting at? You don't want to do this anymore? Just say so. I won't hold you to it. I mean, good grief, if you're going to give me a hard time every time I say let's go to the beach."

"It's just that you just said yourself that things were getting better for you. I thought maybe you're ready to call it quits with our arrangement."

He frowned at me. "When I want out I'll tell you," he said.

Amy shot us a curious look as she passed by.

"She thinks we're having a fight," I said.

"Well, aren't we?"

"No," I said firmly. "We're having a serious discussion, that's all. Well, okay, I'd like to go to the beach if you would. When do you want to go?"

"Pick you up after school. You know, if I didn't know better I'd say you were mad at me for looking at Verena, for Pete's sake."

I snorted. "What an idea!"

We walked on, slowly, in the direction of the classroom building. I struggled with my better self for a moment and lost. "Adam," I said, "doesn't it seem to you that there's something a little . . . odd about Verena?"

"She's different," he said. "Different looking, I mean. Kind of exotic."

I wasn't surprised he had noticed that. As much as he had been looking at her he could have probably given a detailed description of everything about her from the color of the polish on her toenails to the length of her mascara-laden eyelashes.

"It's not just the way she dresses I'm talking about," I said. "You know that roadblock yesterday afternoon?"

"Yeah, the one where they gave you the lecture about seat belts. I got stopped there."

"Everybody got stopped there except Verena. She made a U-turn and tore out of there in the opposite direction."

"No kidding!"

I was pleased that he really seemed interested.

"Wait a minute, though," he said. "Maybe she just had to go back for something or it could be she just didn't want to get held up. I mean, what could some little girl like Verena have to hide from the cops?"

I gave him a nasty look. "I thought you were the one complaining about how girls never got suspected of anything. Just because Verena's a girl, you know, doesn't mean she can't be up to something, too."

"Maybe she's driving without a license?"

"Maybe. Or maybe something worse. Maybe she's *wanted by the police*!"

He grinned. "You've been watching too much television."

We had gotten as far as my chemistry class, so I didn't have time to continue my argument. There might not even be any point in continuing it. Maybe Adam was totally under Verena's spell.

He was still grinning as he took off. "See you later," he said.

I was beginning to wish I hadn't even mentioned my suspicions. It would be awful if he thought I was saying those things just because I was jealous of Verena.

Then an even worse thought struck me. Was it possible that it was true? That the only reason I was suspicious of Verena was because I *was* jealous of her?

As soon as Adam finished his detention work that afternoon, he came by the house to pick me up for the beach. I was wearing shorts and a shirt over my swimsuit.

"Are you going out with Adam again?" Mother asked, looking at me dubiously as I gathered up a towel and beach bag.

"Just to the beach," I said. "I'm ahead on all my school work, Mom, I promise."

"But you don't even like the beach, Mary Ann. When are you going to do some of the things *you* like to do, darling? Believe me, it's a mistake to subordinate your individuality to another person like this. It worries me to see you doing this. It really does."

"It's just the beach, Mom. Not a major life decision. Oops, there he is. See you."

I ran out to Adam's car. I had been worried that he might still be thinking I was jealous of Verena, but the grin he gave me as I got in swept away all my uneasiness. You had to hand it to Adam, he was usually good company. He was not the kind of person who went into the sulks for no reason at all or else insisted on telling you in boring detail about what was wrong with his car.

We went down Indian River Drive in companionable silence and drove north, past the Coast Guard station and out over the bridge to Jack Island. It was a beautiful day with those towering clouds in the sky that are luminously white with dark scalloped edges.

Adam, instead of turning right to take the beach road, turned left. A few moments later he drove into the game preserve parking lot. The parking lot there was a small paved area with the wildness of palmettos and fat sea-grape leaves crowding in on all sides. We walked along the raised, wooden walkway away from the parking lot, moving through a thicket of impenetrable vegetation. After we had gone a ways we came to a bench put there for elderly birdwatchers to rest on. To my surprise, Adam sat down. He was never tired and I was sure the idea of kissing me had never occurred to him, so I was a little curious about why he was sitting down.

Some elderly birdwatchers carrying binoculars appeared and passed by us with a friendly smile. They were thin and wiry and looked rather like birds themselves.

After they had passed, Adam looked up at the sky. "Were you serious about what you said about Verena?" he asked.

"I guess you think it's pretty silly."

"I just wondered why you said it, that's all."

"You don't think it's strange that she avoided that roadblock?"

"Well, maybe. But is that the only thing?"

I thought about it. "It's not that I've noticed anything big," I said. "It's just a lot of little things that don't add up. Like when I was in the office the other day, they were telling her that they'd sent for her records and her old school said they had no record of her."

"Computer foul-up?"

"Maybe. But it didn't seem to bother her a bit. She wasn't even surprised. And when they told her it might take till Christmas to hear from the school again, she seemed to like the idea. Even when Mrs. Meadows told her that they were going to have to get the records before she could graduate, she wasn't a bit rattled. Don't you think a normal person might get a little worried? Here is your old school saying you don't exist, that you never even attended."

"She was very cool, huh?"

"Very."

"You think there's something in her records she doesn't want people to know?"

"I think maybe she doesn't have any records. Not at that school anyway. That's why she wasn't surprised when they didn't send any."

"Why would she want to do something like that?"

"I don't know."

"Maybe it's a custody thing," said Adam. "You said she was living with her father? Maybe she's not supposed to be. Maybe they're hiding from her mother. You're always reading about things like that."

"Not with sixteen-year-old kids," I said. "And that's another thing. I don't think Verena's father looks much like a father."

Adam looked surprised. "What are you getting at?"

"Well, he doesn't look all that old to me. I mean, I guess it's *possible* he's old enough to be her father, all right, but my father looks older than him and I'll bet your father does, too. Also he never seems to go off to work. He doesn't even dress like a father. He wears these little canvas espadrilles with no socks and white linen pants."

"Maybe he works at home."

"Maybe, but another thing is they play this loud music all the time. Have you ever heard of a father that likes loud music playing all the time?"

"Maybe he was in the artillery corps and got some ear damage," said Adam. "Maybe it doesn't sound loud to him."

"Oh, you can think up an explanation for any of it, but when you look at it all together, it just tells me that something's not quite right."

"You don't think you're kind of letting your imagination run away with you?"

"And he always wears sunglasses. Always."

"Contact lens wearer?"

"Or criminal?" I countered. I told him about the man in the striped T-shirt that Verena and her father had seemed to be trying to avoid. "And he was carrying a suitcase," I concluded darkly.

Adam grinned. "Okay, give it to me. What's the sinister meaning of a suitcase?"

I stood up. "All right, make fun of me. When the police come in and arrest them all, then we'll see."

A shadow passed over us and I looked up to see a large bird lighting on a bare branch. "Sea eagle," said Adam softly. "Let's go on down to the creek."

We proceeded down the boardwalk quite a distance, passing a community of wood storks that seemed to stare sourly at us like disapproving preachers, until finally the boardwalk petered out into a path that went along a stream. A couple of middle-aged bird watchers were walking in our direction. "Cuckoo!" one of them called triumphantly, checking off something on her list. I wheeled around but didn't see a thing. I decided she was probably making it all up.

"Look here," Adam said. "Raccoon." I knelt beside him, next to the mud along the creek bank.

I looked where he was pointing and saw a small, skinny-looking handprint sunk into the mud. "Do you think we'll get to see a raccoon?" I asked, starting to get interested.

"Not this time of day," he said. "Maybe at sunset or sunrise. Now notice the print. You can always tell raccoons because you can see the fingerlike prints. Easiest print in the world to recognize."

We followed along the creek a bit farther. "Now here's a rabbit," he said, stooping again. "You can tell by the pattern of the tracks. See how it's hopping?"

"A rabbit? Out here?"

"Maybe a marsh rabbit. This is their territory."

"Look here!" I said, excited that I had spotted a track all by myself. "Look at this little bitty track here."

Adam knelt down beside me. "Good," he said. "Notice this little line? That's its tail dragging behind it. And see this little tapered dropping?"

"Well, what kind of animal is it?"

"Rat."

"A rat!" I said indignantly.

"Yeah, this is a great place to raise rat families. Lots of cover, running water, plenty of birds' eggs to eat."

I shuddered, imagining beady eyes hiding under the sea-grape leaves.

He grinned. "You get disgusted too easy, Mary Ann. The outdoors doesn't come served up on a silver plate."

A blue jay squawked and flew over our heads. I jumped when I heard an ominous rustle in the bushes.

Adam stood up. "Ready to go on over to the beach?" he asked.

"Yes!" I said promptly. It struck me then that Adam looked completely in his element surrounded by mud, sea-grape bushes with a tree behind him dripping ropy vines. He looked like an Indian. Out here was just where he liked to be. No wonder the idea of military school had thrown him into such a panic. Military schools are probably pretty short on wildlife, beaches and woods.

After we left the preserve, we drove to the beach. In no time, we had stripped off our outside clothes and were running into the surf. I fell down and got sand in my swimsuit and salt water in my nose, but felt perfectly happy. I even started laughing. Adam waded over to me, the waves beating against his legs, his wet body gleaming darkly in the afternoon sun. "You okay?" he called.

I got up and pushed the hair out of my face. "Sure," I said.

He raised his voice to compete with the breakers. "You know what we ought to do?" he asked. "We ought to investigate. We ought to investigate Verena."

I anxiously glanced around us but the beach was deserted except for a man far away who was walking his dog. The ocean surged around my feet. "Oh, Verena," I said. "I guess so." For a minute there I had forgotten all about Verena. It struck me that maybe that was why I had been so happy.

Chapter Six

When Adam and I got back to my house, I noticed as soon as I got out of the car that there was no loud music playing from Verena's house. I looked over there and saw that neither of the two cars was there. What's more, a large, green delivery truck pulled up to the house.

"Look, Adam!" I hissed. "Look over there at Verena's house."

He leaned on the steering wheel and glanced in that direction. "So? It's a delivery truck."

I pulled my towel more tightly around my wet swim suit. "But see what it says? It says, Brandon's—Vero Beach. Why would they get Brandon's to deliver something from Vero when there's a branch of the store right here in town?''

"Maybe it's something the local store didn't have?" he suggested.

The truck backed out of the driveway, leaving a large square cardboard package by the front door.

"Nobody's home," I said, glancing at the house. "I think I'll just go over there and take a look at the package."

"Good grief, Mary Ann, you aren't exactly dressed for detective work," he said, glancing at me.

I pushed the wet hair out of my way and quickly dug my sandals out of my beach bag and put them on my gritty feet. "Would Philip Marlowe let a wet swim suit stop him?" I asked. "Would Sherlock Holmes?"

"Probably," said Adam. But he opened the car door and got out.

I waited until the delivery truck was out of sight, then I started across the street.

"Sometimes I wonder about you," Adam said as he followed me. "What if somebody sees us doing this?"

"Nobody'll see us. Practically nobody is home. This is a very quiet neighborhood."

Adam cast a glance down the street. "I just hope Verena doesn't come home and catch us at it."

"We should check and see if the package needs to be taken in," I said virtuously. "It might rain. Or maybe it's something perishable. I'm only being a good neighbor."

Adam let out a whoop, and then looked as if he were sorry about making the noise.

"It's a big package," I said, as we came up to the front of the house.

I was prepared to rip the box open with my fingernails to see what was in it, but luckily that wasn't necessary. It was clearly labeled in bold black letters, Sump Pump. Brandon's Finest.

"What's a sump pump?" I asked.

Adam took my arm and began guiding me back across the street. "Let's talk about it after we get back to your house," he said.

When we were once more standing beside his car, he seemed to breathe more easily.

"A sump pump is something you use to pump water out of something," he said. "Like if you have a basement that leaks or something."

"Well, that can't be what they need it for. The Peebles don't have a basement. Who ever even heard of a basement around here?"

The water table was so high in our part of the world and the soil so light that basements were tricky and expensive to build. Only major public buildings had them.

Then I saw Verena's car driving up. "That package is too heavy for her to move by herself," I murmured. "She'll have to wait for that guy she lives with to come home to move it."

"I wish you wouldn't call him 'that guy,'" said Adam. "He's probably just Verena's dad." He was getting back into his car.

"Then what's the sump pump for?"

"You've got me there," he said. He shot a glance back across the street. The front door was just closing behind Verena.

"I wish we'd got a look at the capacity of that pump," Adam said. "Maybe that would give us a clue about what it could be used for. Tell you what. Maybe I'll ask around a little bit. Try to find out about sump pumps."

"Then we really *are* going to investigate?" I asked.

"It can't hurt to find out what we can. You ought to try to get really chummy with Verena and to find out more about her. Maybe she'd let something slip."

My hands fell helplessly to my side. "I can't," I said simply. "I just cannot get chummy with her."

"The intrepid detective not up to a little sneakiness, huh?" he grinned. "Okay, don't worry. Maybe I can get chummy with her."

He backed his car out of the driveway and drove off. "Great!" I said to myself. "Just what I wanted—Adam getting chummy with Verena."

I went inside sensing that somehow I had made a serious misstep.

Adam wasted no time putting his plan into effect. The next day at school, I had to eat lunch with Lisa. Adam had taken his tray over to the other side of the cafeteria and was tactlessly horning in on a tête-à-tête between Billy Menlo and Verena.

"Is anything wrong?" Lisa asked me anxiously as I sat down beside her and unfolded my tiny paper napkin.

"What could be wrong?" I asked.

"I just wondered if you and Adam had a fight or something."

"No," I said flatly.

"I didn't mean to be nosy or anything," said Lisa, looking at me with wide eyes.

"So we're not eating lunch together. We don't have to eat lunch together every day of the world, you know. Eating lunch together is not such a big deal. People shouldn't cut themselves off completely from the rest of the world just because they happen to be going together."

"Excuse me," said Lisa meekly. "I didn't mean anything."

I ate my meat loaf in silence. Finally Lisa said, "What do you think about that chemistry test? You think it'll be multiple choice?"

"Who cares?" I said.

Lisa swallowed. "You know, you and I ought to try to get together more often. It's really great to see you."

I was conscious that I was not being very good company. "It's just that Verena gets to me so much," I said, gritting my teeth. "I cannot stand her."

"I understand," said Lisa, looking at me sympathetically. "I know it's tough."

"Not that there's anything between Adam and Verena," I added quickly. "It's just that I don't like him *near* her. It sets my teeth on edge."

"Of course," said Lisa, her eyes brimming with sympathy.

Amy and Larry passed by, carrying their trays. Amy paused, bent over and whispered in my ear, "Don't worry, Mary Ann. He'll come back to you."

I ground my teeth and the moment Amy had left, I jumped up. I had completely lost my appetite. As I dumped my barely touched trayful of food into the trash, it occurred to me that this was a great way to lose ten pounds. Too bad that I didn't need to lose ten pounds.

I didn't see Adam again until after school. Then he suddenly appeared at my side in the school parking lot. "Tonight I buy you dinner," he said.

"What is it?" I asked. "What did you find out?"

"Nothing much. But she kept sidestepping my questions. It's fishy, all right." His eyes narrowed. "Billy was awfully anxious to get rid of me, too," he said. "I wonder if he's in on it."

"He just wanted you to get away from Verena. That's all." I could just imagine Billy's reaction when a big hunk of competition like Adam sat down at the table with them.

Adam hit his hand against my car with a re-sounding thump. "Pick you up at six," he said.

"Going out with Adam again?" said Mom plaintively, later that day.

With my toothbrush, I gave my eyebrows a slight upward sweep. I noticed the bridge of my nose was pink from the sun at the beach the day before. Like many people whose families have lived in Florida for generations, I normally avoided the sun. My skin just wasn't prepared for all these Adam-type outdoor activities.

"We're just going to have dinner, Mom. I have to eat."

"You don't have to see Adam every day. You were out with him yesterday."

I looked at her in surprise. "We have a lot to talk about. That's all." I heard his car driving up outside. "Gotta go, Mom."

Adam got out of the car to open the door for me. He was wearing a red knit shirt which was absolutely smashing with his dark hair and his deep tan. It was easy for me to see why Billy Menlo had started having heart palpitations when Adam sat down next to Verena. He really was attractive. I got in the car.

"I thought we'd go to the Sailfish," he said, slipping into the driver's seat. "Okay with you?"

"You must really be convinced I'm onto something with Verena if you're going to treat me to dinner at the Sailfish," I said.

"Can't a guy take his girl out to dinner?" He grinned. "No, seriously, I admit I think you must be onto something."

Since it was a weeknight, there weren't many people in the Sailfish restaurant. Adam and I took a table by the window and ordered the catch of the day. Out on the bridge pilings, three brown pelicans were looking down their beaks with that very serious expression pelicans have. Farther out on the water a pelican was flying high, with powerful strokes of his big wings, looking for fish below. Suddenly he dropped like a lead weight. There was a splash as he hit the water at great speed. A second later, he lifted off and began gaining height once more, his glistening prey held tight in his beak.

Adam was not watching the pelicans. "That girl has got to be hiding something," he said. "I would say that the type of person Verena is would normally be real keen to talk about herself."

"Oh, she is," I said. "You should have heard her when I was interviewing her for that essay in English class. She thinks she's fascinating."

"Yeah. You have the feeling she must spend hours looking in the mirror every day. What do you call it? Narcissistic. Know what I mean?"

I knew what he meant, all right.

"But when I started asking her about where she grew up, what her father did for a living, what her old school was like, she was very slippery, like she didn't want to tell me anything about herself."

"Did she just refuse to answer you?"

"Well, when I asked her what her father did, she said he was a consultant. What kind of a consultant? I asked. Medical supplies consultant, she said. But I had the feeling she was making it up as she went along. And when I started to try to pin her down about her background, she just laughed and said she was sure I didn't want to hear about anything so boring and she started talking about English class. It wasn't a really convincing performance."

I could see that Adam had been far from subtle in his questions. Even somebody as confident of her attractions as Verena must have thought it was odd when he swooped down on her like a hungry pelican and started giving her the third degree. But he had found out that she seemed to be hiding something. That was the important thing.

"Of course, it's possible," I said uncertainly, "that she's just hiding something personal. Unhappy home life or something like that."

"You think?"

"I don't know. Looks to me as if she'd seem more upset if it were something like that."

"Right. She doesn't seem upset."

"She seems smug," I said.

"You've hit it," he agreed.

The waiter appeared with our snapper. Since I absolutely adore red snapper with fresh lemon juice and since Adam was always starving, there was a momentary lull in the conversation while we attacked our food.

Eventually, however, I wiped my buttery lips and turned my attention back to our problem. "The sump pump," I said.

"I asked around," said Adam. "You can use them for draining cesspools."

"What's a cesspool?"

"Sort of a septic tank. They aren't allowed in the city limits. The fact is, they don't work very well.

Nobody I know has ever heard of anybody having one. You might find one in an old farmhouse or something. Maybe."

"That's out, then."

"And you're sure the Peebleses don't have a basement."

"The idea's laughable. You know the way it is around here. You dig down twenty feet and you've got yourself a well, not a basement."

He looked at me. "Hey! I think you've got something! They must be digging," he said.

I thought about it. "I haven't seen any signs of digging," I said.

"You aren't home all day. That guy could be digging in the backyard while you're in school. I'd like to poke around over there some and try to find out."

"Why would they be digging in their backyard? They don't even own the house. The Peebleses wouldn't be too happy to come back and find out they've dug up the backyard."

"So what? Maybe by then Verena and her dad plan to be long gone," he said. "Particularly, if they're after *buried* treasure!" I grinned. "Oh, come on now. Gold doubloons and pieces of eight?"

"Did I laugh at you when you came telling me there was something fishy about Verona?"

"Yes," I said.

"Look, a lot of boats went all up and down along this coast," he said, ignoring me. "Spanish ships, pirates, privateers. Nobody can be sure what's buried where. You know people sometimes do dig up treasure. Look at that stuff that's in the state museum out on Jack Island."

"I know they have some gold doubloons there," I admitted slowly. "But if Verena and that guy think they're onto buried treasure, why the secrecy? Wouldn't they want help? Wouldn't they want backers for the excavation?"

"I can think of one good reason for the secrecy," Adam said. "Look at that treasure hunter, Mel Fisher, that brought up a ship full of emeralds down near Key West. What do you think is circling that ship of emeralds down there all the time?"

"The Coast Guard?"

"Right. The government gets the first bite and it's a big one for sure."

"I see what you mean. You might double your take if you didn't have to pay taxes on it."

"That's it. Tell you what. I'm going to go over to Verena's tomorrow and do some poking around. See what I can find."

"Wouldn't that look suspicious? Maybe I should go. I could be just paying a friendly neighborly call."

"You think Verena's going to believe you're paying a neighborly call?" he asked, looking at me sideways.

"I guess not," I had to admit. "Not unless she's very stupid and if you can believe her, she has an IQ of a hundred and thiry-five."

"No kidding, did she really say that?"

"You've talked to her. You ought to know I'm not making it up. But why should she believe that *you're* paying a neighborly call? I'll bet you've already made her suspicious by asking her all those questions at lunch."

He pulled something out of his pocket and laid it on the table. I looked at it as if hypnotized. It was a delicate French purse-style wallet of snake skin with a jeweled clasp. I was appalled to see that the jewels looked real.

"I got it out of her pocketbook when she wasn't looking."

I shot him an anxious glance, then reached for it.

"Don't bother," he said. "I checked. There's no driver's license, no credit cards. Nothing but a hundred dollars cash."

"What if you get arrested for taking it?" I squeaked.

He put it back in his pocket. "I thought we agreed Verena didn't want to attract the attention of the police," he said. "Besides, I'm going to return it, the way any honest person would. That's going to be my neighborly call."

"And you're going to go up to their back door? Won't that look kind of funny?"

"Not if I arrive by boat," he said with a smug smile. "I'll just pull right up to the dock and go up to the house the back way. Perfectly natural."

"Golly, I hope it doesn't make her suspicious," I said uneasily. I hadn't really intended to launch a full-scale detective operation when I had told him about my feelings about Verena. It's one thing to have little fantasies about your neighbors and something else entirely to actually *do* something about them.

It did not add to my peace of mind when, as we drove home in the waning light, I saw Adam cast a glance up at the city water tower. "Class of '84," he said in disgust. "Can you believe nobody has brought that thing up to date?"

I covered my eyes with my hand. "I think there are good reasons for that," I said. "The height of the tower, for one. The alertness of the police, for another." It was occurring to me that Adam wasn't so completely different from his brothers as he liked to make out.

"Aw, it's not so high if you know what you're doing," he said. "And the police can't watch it every night. Besides, they aren't expecting anybody to paint it this year. Nobody touched it the last two years. They've forgotten all about it.''

"You ought to forget all about it, too," I said.

He pulled up into our driveway and reached across to open the door for me. "Heck, just think, Mary Ann. If you'd never clued me in to Verena, this would be just another dull week."

That was awfully smart of me, I thought.

"Maybe the Feds will give us an award or something," he said. "You know, if you turn in an income tax cheat, you get a cut of the take. If we're really onto what we think we're onto, it's sort of the same kind of thing. Hey, just imagine, we could be on the trail of buried treasure!"

Right, I thought as I got out of the car. Adam could also be on his way to jail. On the whole, that felt more likely to me at the moment than heaps of gold doubloons and pieces of eight.

Chapter Seven

Adam figured Verena would be sleeping late on Saturday, but I knew he planned to return her wallet sometime after ten, as soon as he could get his boat over there. I also knew I'd be a nervous wreck by then.

A thick bunch of cabbage palms stood blocking my view of Verena's backyard, but this did not stop me from peering outside anyway. I had rolled our jalousied windows open so I could hear what was going on outside, but all was quiet except for the papery rustle as a breeze touched a palm near the window. "Everything is so quiet," I said fretfully to Mom. "It's spooky. You'd think nobody lived in this neighborhood."

"You wouldn't be far wrong," she said, looking up from her book. "The Coopers and the Michaelsons don't get here till November and the Fullers left for the Keys a week ago. Right now there's just us, the Stuarts and the new neighbors."

"I didn't know the Fullers had already gone. Did they ask you to keep an eye on the house for them?"

"You must be kidding, sweetheart. Don't you remember when they put in that state-of-the-art burglar alarm system last year? If even a mouse crosses their threshold, a bell goes off at police headquarters. I believe it's all done with invisible rays or something. Louella told me it was the most comprehensive, most advanced, most foolproof system available. The systems engineers were out here for days setting it up and checking it out. Goodness, to ask me to keep an eye on their house would be like admitting that all that money they spent on it was wasted."

This talk about burglar alarm systems was doing nothing for my nerves. I sat down and picked up a book and stared at it sightlessly for what seemed like forever. What was happening across the street? I would have given a lot to know, but I didn't dare go out and try to find out. If Verena saw me snooping around, that really would look suspicious.

Finally, I couldn't stand it any longer. I threw down the book and jumped up from my chair.

"I didn't realize you were interested in Nietzsche, darling!" Mom said in a pleased voice. "I was going to ask you to help me fold clothes, but you seemed to be so absorbed in your reading, I didn't like to interrupt you." She reached toward the bookshelves. "I have a commentary here that you may find helpful," she said.

"I've got to go call Adam right now," I said, escaping to my room.

After I dialed the number, Adam's phone seemed to ring forever, but finally, the receiver was picked up. "'Lo," Adam said.

"Is that you? Are you all right?" I asked.

"Sure, I'm all right. I'm just out of breath because I ran in the house when I heard the phone ringing that's all."

"Well, what did you find out? Tell me!"

"Not much," he admitted. "I poked around some in back of their place. First I searched really well around the dock and along the path that goes up the bank to the yard. There's a lot of undergrowth there and it would be pretty easy to hide any digging you were doing if you covered it over with brush."

"But there they'd be in full sight of any boats going along the waterway!" I protested.

"Not if they did the work at night," he said. "But I didn't find anything. So that was a washout. Then I went up into the yard and looked around. I even checked the storage shed, but it was locked and I couldn't break into it without making a lot of noise. There wasn't sign of any digging anywhere. Then, Verena came to the back door and saw me."

"Do you think she saw you searching the yard?"

"She must have. Or else why would she come to the back door?"

"What did you say?"

"Not much. Just said, 'Nice place you've got here.' Told her I'd been looking around."

"You really think Verena's going to believe you're that interested in real estate?" I asked impatiently. "What did she say when you gave her back her wallet?"

"Thanks. What else could she say?"

"She *must* be suspicious."

"Maybe. But so what? What's she going to do about it?" he asked.

Monday, at lunch, Adam was in a terrific mood. In spite of everything I had said, he wasn't a bit disturbed about the possibility that he had aroused Verena's suspicions. "Maybe it'll stir them up a little bit," he said. "Maybe Verena will get rattled and let something slip." A faraway look came into his eyes. "I used to dream about buried treasure when I was a little kid," he said. "I had a book called *Famous Pirates*. I can't say I much liked the pirates. Some of them were real psycho cases, creeps like you wouldn't believe. But the buried treasure—golly, can't you see it? The gold doubloons, the uncut emeralds, the pearls dripping over the chest lid and a silver chalice sticking up here and there. Let's face it, there's something just fantastic about buried treasure."

"Okay, I can see it's got more appeal than stocks and bonds," I said sourly. "But I don't see that we're any closer to finding out about it than we ever were."

"I still think they might get rattled and give something away now that they know we're onto them, but if we don't get anywhere in the next week or so, maybe I could break into that storage shed or into their house and see what I could find."

"Break into their house?" I asked, appalled. "I thought you wanted to stay out of jail."

"Okay, maybe breaking in is going a little far," he said, opening another milk carton. "Let's just say we give it some time and see what happens. This is really something, though, isn't it," he said happily. "Just thinking about it sort of adds zip to your day, if you know what I mean. I feel like a different person than when I was spending all my time walking on tippy toes, trying to stay out of trouble."

"Staying out of trouble is a good thing," I reminded him.

"Oh, sure," he said.

But I didn't feel he was really paying attention to what I said. I was afraid that this business of being on the track of buried treasure had stirred up the renegade Kincaid blood in him. My suspicion was confirmed by what he said next.

"Anyway," he added, "it's not like I have to sit around just holding my hands until things break on the treasure case. I'm giving some serious thought to painting that water tower."

I clutched my fork in a tight grip. "Oh, no, Adam! Don't! It's not safe."

"Just because you have to get up high to do something doesn't mean it's not safe," he said patiently. "You just use an extension ladder to get to the first level of the tower and after that it's more or less a piece of cake."

It was the "less" part that was bothering me. "When are you thinking about doing it?" I asked. My mind was racing. I was already thinking how I would go to the city maintenance people and suggest that it was time to repaint the water tower. I could put it to them that as a public service they might as well repaint it with the slogan "Class of

'87" instead of a simple olive drab. That would stop Adam from going through with this crazy idea.

He finished off his second carton of milk. "Tomorrow night," he said.

"Tomorrow night!" I gasped.

"Keep your voice down. I don't want everybody and his brother to know about it," he said. "Yes, tomorrow. This is perfect weather for it—clear skies, full moon. I've already picked up the paint I'll need. By one a.m. the moon will be up and everybody will be off the streets. That's when I'll do it."

"I don't think this is a good idea, Adam."

He grinned. "Don't worry about it. Anything Steve and Mark can do, I can do. Believe me."

"You're the first person they'll suspect."

"Me? You got to be kidding. By now I've got a whole new reputation. Mr. Jansen even told me he thought I should give some thought to majoring in history in college. How about that?"

"Why take the risk?" I asked, almost whimpering now. "It's taken you so long to get out from under your brothers' reputation. Why throw it all away like this?"

"Don't you see, Mary Ann? If I do it and don't get caught, I'll be one up on Steve and Mark. I'll have done it even better than they did."

I gave up then. I hadn't been a younger kid myself for sixteen years without getting some insight into how competition between kids in the same family works. If he were determined to outdo Steve and Mark, I knew it was hopeless to try to persuade him.

But I wasn't anything like as sure as he was that he wouldn't get caught. When we got up from the lunch table a bunch of boys I didn't know came up and slapped him on the back. I didn't hang around to hear exactly what they were saying, but the ominous word "tower" floated in my direction. It was pretty clear that I wasn't the only person who knew what Adam had in mind. In fact, I realized, there would be no point in painting the tower anonymously. There would be no glory in it. Half the boys in school knew about it already. All it would take for big trouble would be for one of them to call the cops.

When I got home from school, Lisa phoned. "I hear Adam's going to paint the water tower tonight," she said.

I groaned.

"Is something the matter?"

"Everything," I said. "How did you hear about it?"

"Larry told me. Everybody knows."

"Is Larry going to go with Adam?" I asked hopefully. Larry was so cautious, I knew he would try to keep Adam from doing anything *too* risky.

"Are you kidding? Larry's parents would kill him if they caught him doing anything like that. Don't you remember how the Kincaid boys got thrown in jail for doing it a couple of years ago? Besides, it's not safe. Some kids in Binghamton tried it last year and one fell down and broke his back. I heard he was in a body cast for months. He was lucky he wasn't killed."

"Did you just call to cheer me up?" I asked tartly. "Or did you have something else you wanted to tell me?"

"Adam told Larry he doesn't want any help. Strictly a one-man proposition. That's the way he wants it."

He is absolutely out of his mind, I thought. He could fall out there and nobody would even know anything was wrong until morning. He could die!

"What did you say?" said Lisa.

"Nothing. I must have groaned again. I seem to be groaning a lot lately."

"Well, it is a little bit of excitement for a change," said Lisa. "All Larry does these days is worry about whether he'll get into a decent college or not. His idea of a fine evening is curling up with his solid geometry book."

"Larry is very sensible."

"Oh, sure. Well, I hope everything goes all right. I mean, you know, I hope Adam doesn't fall and break his back or get arrested or anything," she said blithely.

That night I went to bed at eleven, the way I always do, but there was no hope of my getting to sleep. I just lay there staring at the ceiling but seeing Adam writhing on the ground.

I had even worked myself up to wishing that the police would be waiting for him when he got there. Better arrested than dead, I thought.

The time dragged by. Slowly I became aware that the venetian blinds were casting a shadow on the wall beside my bed. The moon was up. I squinted at my wristwatch and was able to make out that it was almost one o'clock. The house was completely quiet. Mom and Dad had been in bed for hours.

I jumped up and started dressing, quickly pulling on jeans and a sweatshirt. I had decided that anything was better than lying there thinking of all the awful things that could happen to Adam. Now that I had made up my mind to go check on him, I moved as fast as I could, but instead of slipping on my sandals, I did take the time to lace up tennis shoes. I knew they would be better for sneaking soundlessly out of the house.

When I opened the door to the hall the hinges squeaked and I stopped dead in my tracks but to my relief Dad's snoring continued uninterrupted down the hall. The living room was full of moving shadows, cast by the moonlight shining through the bougainvillea vine outside.

I crept out our front door and once outside quickly jumped in my car and locked all its doors.

A moment later I was driving toward the water tower. I only passed a few cars. Adam had been right. By this hour, the streets were pretty much deserted. After a few minutes I saw the water tower looming ahead, gray in the moonlight.

I parked my car beside a storage shed near the foot of the tower. I didn't like being out in the run-down area near the train tracks alone at night, but I was safe, I told myself, as long as I stayed in my locked car. The trouble was, I couldn't really see anything from my car. I could make out the shape of the water tower against the sky, but closer to the ground the shadows of buildings cast everything near them into deep darkness. Where could Adam be?

I heard a train rumbling over its tracks a couple of blocks away and somewhere not too far away a dog barked. Encouraged by those sounds of life, I got out of the car and took a few cautious steps. Then all at once I heard the crunching sound of a shoe on gravel not far from me. My heart leapt to my throat and stayed there beating fiercely. I froze, glad I was not far from my car. If some derelict were skulking in the shadows, I could still get away.

Then, up on the water tower I saw Adam's dark shape moving along the narrow railed rim of the tower. Whose footsteps had I heard? I frantically surveyed the scene, only sketchily lit by the moon. There was no sign of Adam's car or of any police cars, just piles of boxes and metal drums ten or fifteen feet ahead of me, a large piece of earthmoving equipment parked over to my left and large washes of black shadow where I could make out nothing. Any number of depraved derelicts could have been hiding there for all I could see.

Then I saw something that made me go rigid. Jutting up from the oil drums and silhouetted against the rising moon was the black shape of a rifle barrel. My throat felt suddenly dry.

Meanwhile Adam inched his way carefully along the narrow railed walkway that circled the tower. He paused and then I saw him lift his arm. I supposed he must have been holding a paintbrush but he was too far away for me to be sure. Then I sensed a movement near the oil drums and suddenly a shot like a sharp explosion rang out near me.

I screamed as I saw Adam stumble. I stooped and picked up the first thing that came to my hand, a tire iron at my feet on the gravel. I threw it, hard, at one of the oil drums. It hit with a clang and another shot exploded.

For the first time, it occurred to me that there was nothing to stop the rifleman from shooting *me*. I shrank back against the storage shed, hiding in its shadow. As I pressed my body against it, something hard in the pockets of my jeans poked into my flesh. It was the whistle I had taken from the Merton twins when I was baby-sitting with them.

I pulled it with trembling fingers from my pocket, put it to my lips and blew so hard my ears hurt. A gratifyingly loud, shrill whistle rent the air. I quickly blew it again, hard, and then I heard the sound of running footsteps on gravel. A moment later, I heard a car starting up on the other side of the storage bin. There was the sound of scattering gravel as its tires spun and took off. I let a sigh of relief escape me. I had managed to scare the gunman away.

But, when I lifted my eyes to look at the water tower, my heart stopped when I saw that Adam's dark form was prone and motionless on the narrow walkway. For an awful moment, I was afraid he had been hit. Then he moved and I knew he couldn't be seriously hurt. He seemed to be creeping cautiously along the walkway.

I ran toward the tower. "Adam!" I screamed. "Are you all right?"

I climbed partway up the extension ladder and saw that he was climbing down toward me. His white teeth flashed in the shadows when he reached the steel girders just above me. "I knew you didn't want me to do it, Mary Ann," he said. "But don't you think shooting at me is carrying opposition a little bit too far?"

"Idiot! It wasn't me. Somebody over by the oil drums was shooting at you."

He peered in the direction of the storage shed. "Is he gone?"

"I guess so. I heard his car driving away."

"Where are the cops?"

"There aren't any cops. What are you talking about?"

"Didn't you hear that police whistle?"

I held up the whistle. "That was me." The moonlight glinted on it, a stout metal whistle about two inches long. "Nice and loud. I took it away from the Merton twins last week."

"God bless the Merton twins," he said. "Well, I don't think that guy's going to try anything again tonight, do you? I'd better get back up there and finish my painting."

"You've got to be kidding!"

"Want to help me? It'd go faster that way."

"He might have gone back for help!" I said.

"Won't take me long." He scampered up the metal ladder again.

"Adam Kincaid," I yelled as he climbed up again, "you are crazy. You are out of your ever-loving mind! This is sibling rivalry gone mad, I tell you. If you had the sense God gave a clam you'd get down from there right now and go home!''

He paused a moment after he got to the walkway and yelled down, ''Heck, Mary Ann, I didn't know you cared!''

Grinding my teeth, I climbed down from the extension ladder and sat on the cold ground while dew collected on the metal girders near me and Adam painted ''Class of '87'' on the water tower.

When he came down, carrying a can of paint and a paintbrush, I refused to speak to him and began silently walking toward my car.

''I'm parked a block away,'' he said. ''I didn't want to put the car where it could be identified in case the police showed up.''

I continued walking.

''Come on, Mary Ann. Think about it a minute. I *had* to finish painting the tower. If I didn't everybody was going to ask me why and what was I going to tell them? That I got shot at?''

I spoke between clenched teeth. ''You'd better tell somebody you got shot at. Namely the police. Some nut with a rifle is running around out there and it's up to them to stop him.''

''Nope. Can't do that. You see how mad you are? That's because you got scared. It always happens that way. It's a sort of reaction to being scared, you see. If my parents found out about this, just like you, first they'd be scared, then they'd be so mad they couldn't see straight and they'd ship me straight off to one of those schools. And what about you? You want to tell your parents where you were tonight?''

I was beginning to see his point. "But it's our public duty,'' I protested. ''You can't let freakos go around shooting at people and getting away with it. The police have got to find out who it was and lock him up.''

''Oh, we know who it was.''

I looked at him blankly.

''Don't you remember,'' he said, ''when I said that we might be stirring things up a bit?''

''You mean Verena or her dad? You think they were shooting at you?''

''I think so,'' he said thoughtfully. ''In fact, I'm sure of it.''

Chapter Eight

The next day, after school, Adam and I drove to the city beach on Hunter Island. I had overruled Jack Island beach. "Too isolated," I said flatly. "Too wooded up behind the beach. I want lots of people around and plenty of clear space so I can see people coming."

"You're getting awfully jumpy aren't you?"

"Only idiots aren't jumpy when people are shooting at them," I said. I noticed he didn't really argue with me. He must have been pretty shaken up by that gunfire himself.

I took off the big shirt that covered up my swimsuit, stuffed it inside my towel and sat down in a warm shallow tidal pool. There were plenty of people on the beach, but no one was very near us. I checked the horizon where in a band of dark blue the sea met the sky and was relieved to see that no ships bristling with cannons were bearing down on us. The parking lot had contained no armored tanks, and the swimsuits worn by the people around us wouldn't have concealed a fountain pen, let alone a gun. I decided I felt relatively safe.

"I still think we should tell the police," I said, scooping up a handful of wet sand.

"We've been all over that," said Adam. "Even if we told the police, why should they believe us? What evidence do we have? Can we show them a bullet? Can we give them a description of the car? We've got nothing."

I began methodically building a sand castle. Adam bent over and began helping me, digging out a moat.

"We've got them cornered," he said, curving the moat around the east end of my castle. "They must be awfully worried or they wouldn't have shot at me."

"Well, *I'm* worried. You don't seem to realize you could have been killed." A little wave washed up and filled the moat with water.

Adam kept digging. "A miss is as good as a mile," he said. "I think we must be getting close to finding out something."

"I think you're crazy," I said. "We don't have a single, solid clue." I dribbled wet sand on my foundation to make ice-cream-cone-shaped towers.

I looked at my castle disconsolately. I now realized why medieval folk had built these things to begin with. It was because people were shooting at them. I wished now that I lived in one myself. Complete with moat. "I'd stay home from school and keep all my doors locked," I said, "but Mr. Stuart, the truant officer, would be after me in a minute. Why did I have to live next to a truant officer?"

"You're taking a defeatist attitude, Mary Ann," he said. "You've lost your nerve."

"You're right," I said. "I have." I burrowed my hand under the sand, making a short little tunnel into my castle, firming the sand all around it before I carefully drew my hand out. Making these tunnels in the sand had been a favorite occupation of mine when I was little. I noticed it didn't give me quite the same kick as it had when I was six.

"We just watch them, wait and see what they do next," Adam said.

"The thing they do next may be to kill you."

When we finally left the beach, we drove past the water tower. "Stop," I said. "Let's just look around. Maybe we'll find a rifle shell or something and if we do, let's go to the police."

He pulled up next to the storage shed where I had parked the night before. Even by daylight, the place gave me the creeps now.

"I'm not saying I'll go to the police," he said. "But okay, I see it wouldn't hurt to find some evidence. Where do you think the guy was standing?"

I got out of the car and showed him. Some of the heavy equipment had been moved, but otherwise, nothing seemed to be changed from the night before. I saw that oil had been spilled near the big metal drums and I walked over to the dark stain it had left on the ground. "Look!" I said. There at the edge of the oil spill was a footprint. I was sure it was the mark of a crinkle-soled espadrille. "The track of a rat," I said sourly.

In the end we gave up on finding any trace of a bullet. "Needle in a haystack," pronounced Adam, and I had to agree with him. It was hopeless. I couldn't think what to do next.

"At least don't tell anybody where you're going," I said. "Half the school knew you were going to be at the water tower all alone in the middle of the night. Don't make that mistake again. Will you promise me that?"

He grinned. "Well, everybody knows where I'm going to be Saturday night," he said.

"Where?"

"The Fall Frolic, with you. Remember?"

I had forgotten all about it. There's nothing like a couple of rifle shots to take your mind off your social ambitions.

"You're going to feel better after you get some sleep," Adam promised me when he let me out at my house.

My eyes moved irresistibly to Verena's house. A clamor of music was again coming from that direction. "Loud music," I muttered. "What can it mean?"

"Take a nap," advised Adam.

I took a nap and when I woke up, I had to admit that I did feel a little more optimistic. I was still very worried, however. You cannot sleep away gunfire.

Friday afternoon, Amy showed up at the front door with a pink satin dress on a hanger. "Mom just finished it!" she said, sweeping into the house. "I couldn't wait to show it to you." She waltzed around holding it in front of her for a minute. "You see the thin spaghetti straps? Just a touch of the sixties," she said. "But the gathers on the sides of the bodice give it a current look. And see the skirt? Cut on the bias." She laid the dress down on the couch and cooed at it. "Is yours ready? Can I see it?"

I led her back to my bedroom and took my dress out of the closet. "Oh, Mary Ann!" she exclaimed. "Where did you get it? I can't wait to see it on you. It's gorgeous. Golly, it looks pretty low-cut, or is that just the way it is on the hanger?''

"It *is* pretty low-cut," I said, a trace of satisfaction in my voice. The dress, with its filmy skirt and its jeweled straps and, most of all, its excessive price represented a major triumph for me over Mom's misgivings. Only my offer to foot two-thirds of the cost with my savings from baby-sitting had tipped the scales in my favor. It was odd to think now how happy I had been when we walked out of the store with it. At this point I was looking at it critically and thinking that on the whole a bulletproof vest would appeal to me more. I hung it back up in the closet.

"Mona has seen the gym since they got all the decorations up and she says it's heavenly," burbled Amy. "The basketball hoops have been covered up with big pompons of tissue-paper flowers and you can hardly even see the gym mats. It's going to be lovely. Ooo, I can't wait until Larry sees me in my dress! I think I'll put a few flowers in my hair. What do you think?" She swung the dress in front on her, the better to admire the flow of its bias-cut skirt. "Jenny is going with Steve, of course," she went on. "And Tonya's friends fixed her up with that exchange student, Abdul. Too bad he doesn't speak much English. Deanna's made up with David, so they're going together. And guess who Mike Eason asked. Cissie Harper!" She laid her dress carefully over a chair. "I get the feeling you aren't listening to me," she complained.

"I heard every word. Mike Eason, Cissie Harper."

"What's the matter with you? You act like you aren't even interested in the dance."

"Okay, I'm not interested. So, sue me."

"Well, excuse *me* for boring you. It used to be all you could think about was the Fall Frolic. All anybody had to do was to mention it and you turned green from head to toe. What's come over you? You better watch out. You don't want to end up eccentric do you? Like that guy Elton who goes around all the time talking about his basset hounds? Believe me, regular people take an interest in the social life around them. That's what's called having a normal social adjustment. I think you need to work on it."

I could see that I had hurt her feelings. "It's not that you were boring me. It's just that I've got a lot of other things on my mind, that's all."

She immediately went all systems alert. "Is it about you and Adam?" she asked. "Is something bothering you? You can tell me. Maybe you need a little impartial advice. Is Adam getting too serious? Is that it? Is he crowding you?"

The way Amy saw the world as one romance after another was beginning to get to me. If you said Michelangelo painted the Sistine Chapel she'd want to know who he went out with. If you pointed out that Susan B. Anthony helped get the vote for women, Amy'd probably say, "Yeah, but did she have any dates?"

I debated with myself whether to give her the shock of her life by telling her about Adam getting shot at. My internal debate lasted only about a half a minute. If I said the first word about it, I knew Amy would broadcast the news all over town.

"It's college, Amy," I said, fixing her eyes with a serious look. "I'm thinking a lot lately about what kind of college I'll be able to get into. You know, whether my grades are as good as they should be."

"College!" she shrieked. "You're starting to sound like Larry. You've got all year to think about college. Fall Frolic is *Saturday night*. Get your head on straight, Mary Ann."

"Sorry," I said penitently. "I'll try to concentrate on the Frolic."

She looked at me suspiciously. "You know, I hate to tell you but I wouldn't be a bit surprised if you ended up like your mother and started spending all your time reading books about the meaning of life. Eccentric—that's the way you'll end up if you aren't careful."

I didn't say so, but turning eccentric was the least of my worries.

* * *

Ever since Adam had gotten shot at, I had been spending a lot of time peering out my bedroom curtains at Verena's house. If the guy with the sunglasses came out carrying a rifle, I wanted to know about it.

The next morning while I was getting dressed, I kept popping over to the window and taking a peek every few minutes. That was how I happened to see the guy in the sunglasses coming out Saturday morning. I watched him throw an overnight bag in the back seat of his car and drive away. Was he really going away overnight? Was it possible I could breathe easy this evening and not worry about Adam being hit by a sniper shot while we were dancing?

It was only later, while I was getting ready for the dance, that a couple of unpleasant facts dawned on me. First, an overnight bag is no guarantee that somebody is going away overnight. Conceivably, it could have been filled with potato chips and bologna sandwiches and other things to munch on while lying in wait to shoot at Adam. Second, the fact that I didn't see the man carrying a rifle out to the car proved nothing. Who was to say the rifle wasn't already *in* the car?

After I finished dressing, Dad took a picture of me standing by the fireplace in my filmy new dress. When the flashbulb went off I jumped a mile. Then

I heard the doorbell and tottered in that direction with blue dots floating in front of my eyes. It was nice to know, I thought bitterly as I opened the door for Adam, that I would have a snapshot to commemorate the evening I spent as a total nervous wreck.

As we walked out to the car a bit later, Adam said, "I think your mom is starting to give me those suspicious looks. Your dad, too, for that matter. Have they been talking to people?"

"Oh, don't worry," I said. "That's not because of your reputation. They just think we've been seeing too much of each other." I glanced over at Verena's house and noticed that the porch light had been switched on. "Too bad we can't tell them what's going on," I said glumly. "Then they'd *really* worry."

Adam opened the car door for me. "You look terrific in that thing," he said. He gently twanged one of the jeweled straps. "A little something whipped up for you by the Marquis de Sade? Those things must cut like the devil."

I slid into the car. "It is necessary to suffer to be beautiful." I lifted my skirt out of the way as he closed the door.

After he got in the car, I burst out, "Adam, what are we going to do?"

"Go to the dance." He backed out of the driveway.

"You know what I mean! I can't think about anything else but how can we keep that guy from shooting at you? He might try it again."

"I don't know. To tell you the truth, the only thing that's keeping me from worrying is that you're doing enough worrying for the both of us."

"I saw the man leave this morning with an overnight case, and at first I felt better, but then I realized he might just be trying to make it look as if he were leaving. I can't figure out what's going on over there. Nothing is what it seems."

"I'll tell you what bothers me," Adam said, with a wry twist of his mouth. "I know people don't like to pay taxes, but not too many of them are ready to commit murder to get out of it. It's beginning to look to me as if there isn't any buried treasure, after all."

He looked so disappointed I realized that he really had had his heart set on gold doubloons.

When we got to the school, the parking lot around the gym was full of cars. Light beamed out of the high windows of the gym and I could hear music. I took Adam's hand. "Hurry up," I whispered. "Let's get inside where there are people. It's safer."

Inside, a bunch of kids were standing near the punch bowl and a mob was milling around the gym dancing to slow music. Adam and I moved toward the center of the gym and began dancing. I leaned against him, feeling the roughness of his jacket against my cheek. "Isn't it funny," I sniffled, "how things are never the way you think they're going to be?"

Adam fished out his handkerchief and handed it to me. "Did you catch up on your sleep the way I told you to?" he asked. "You seem to be falling apart at the seams."

I blotted my eyes carefully and looked up at him. "I didn't smear my mascara, did I?"

"Nope," he said. He smiled at me. "Don't worry so much, Mary Ann. There's not enough light in here for them to shoot at us."

I hoped he was right. My eyes fell on Verena. She was wearing a long red dress with a corsage of white flowers pinned to the shoulder strap. She and Billy Menlo were dancing together under one of the decorated basketball hoops, imperfectly concealed by a pompon of paper flowers. I grabbed Adam's arm. "Look," I whispered. "It's Verena."

Adam glanced over in that direction. Billy's Adam's apple could be seen moving convulsively and his eyes were bulging slightly as he guided Verena around the basketball hoops. "Will you look at poor old Menlo? Probably overcome by that perfume she wears," Adam observed sympathetically.

Another time, I might have enjoyed these unmistakable signs that Adam's enchantment with

Verena was finished, but at that moment I didn't have time to savor the triumph. "Don't you see?" I asked. "She's *here*."

"I don't follow you."

"I mean, she's not at home. And I'll bet that guy with the sunglasses is gone, too. He did take an overnight case. Don't you see what this means? This is our chance to break into their house."

"Did I hear you right? Did you say break into their house? I thought you were against doing anything that might land us in jail."

"That was before you got shot at," I said impatiently. "Can you think of any better ideas? Are we just going to sit around waiting for him to take another shot at you? We've got to figure out what they're up to and then go to the police. Don't you see?"

"Maybe you're right," he said softly. "Maybe we better grab this chance."

"Let's just dance over casually to the door," I said. "We don't want Verena to see us leaving."

We danced over past the chaperons and in the direction of the door, but we were forced to kill a little time drinking punch at the punch bowl until Verena danced completely out of our sight into the crowd. Then, with a single meaningful glance at each other, we made for the exit.

By the time we got to the car, I felt as if I had a temperature of a hundred and two. "If we ever get out of this business in one piece," I said fervently, "I'll never play detective again."

"I hope we're going to be able to get into the place with no trouble," said Adam. "We aren't exactly dressed for burglary and all I've got in the trunk of the car is just a jack, a rope and a screwdriver. I hope I've got a flashlight." He groped under the seat. "Yep, here it is."

"They've got jalousied windows just like ours," I said. "If we can pry them open with the screwdriver, we can just lift each pane out and then push the screen in."

I was petrified my parents would recognize Adam's car driving up so we parked one street down and began walking to Verena's house. My strappy sandals weren't made for that kind of trek but I gritted my teeth and put up with the pain. Before long, we were standing at the back corner of Verena's house.

My heart gave a little jump of joy when I saw that one of the glass jalousies was already broken. Once we jiggled the broken pane out, it was very simple to lift the remaining jalousies out of their metal clasps.

"I'm afraid I'm not going to be able to climb in the window in this skirt," I said. "You'll have to go."

"You're going to have to be lookout. Now, stand where you can see the street, and if you see either of their cars coming run to this window and shout for me. Better yell something like 'Here, Spot!' That way if anybody hears you it'll sound like you're looking for a dog.''

"All right," I said. "I just hope I can yell anything at all. I'm already so scared I can hardly speak.''

"Don't worry. You yelled fine that night they were shooting. Here I go.''

The window was one of those that are almost shoulder height, but Adam put his hands on the sill and quickly boosted himself up and scrambled through it. I heard his flashlight hit the floor as he went over the sill, but then I saw a faint glow within, so it had survived the fall and was still working.

I ran to the front corner of the house and anxiously watched the street. Across the street I saw the light go on in Mom and Dad's room. It was very odd to feel that they were so close by while I was busy assisting in a burglary. When I thought about how they trusted me, I felt terrible, but when I thought about how that creep had shot at Adam, I didn't see that we had any choice. We had to find out what was going on.

The street remained deserted with no sign of any car. It wasn't long before I heard Adam clambering back over the windowsill. There was a soft thud as he jumped to the ground. I ran back to him.

"Did you find out anything?" I asked breathlessly. "Did you see anything?"

"Hurry up, Mary Ann," he panted. "Get back up there and keep a lookout. We don't want to get caught now. I'm going to try to get the screen and the jalousies back in."

I ran back up to the front corner of the house and watched the road so intently that my eyes started to hurt because I forgot to blink. It seemed to take much longer to put the window back together than it had taken for us to break in.

"I bent the screen," Adam said when he came to get me. "But there's no help for it. Just hope they don't notice. Let's get out of here."

We took a fallen palm frond and swished it across the ground to obscure the mark of our footsteps near the window, then we cut behind the house and hurried back to where we had parked the car.

When we got in the car, Adam let out his breath in a way that made me realize he had been holding it for a while. In the dim light cast by the dashboard I could see that his face looked strained.

"What did you find out?" I asked anxiously as we drove off. "What was in there? You didn't seem to take very long."

"You're never going to believe this," he said heavily. "The place was full of dirt."

"Dirt?" I echoed incredulously. It seemed like an odd time to be criticizing Verena's housekeeping.

"I mean *dirt*," he said. "Earth, soil, dirt—to the ceiling. Rooms full of dirt."

He pulled out on Indian River Drive and turned in the direction of town. I stared uncomprehendingly at the road ahead. "Dirt?"

"They're camping out in just a couple of rooms," he said. "The living room is okay, and that bedroom we broke into is clear, but the rest of the rooms are *full to the ceilings with dirt*!"

"Golly, the Peebleses are really going to be ticked off when they get back and find it that way," I said.

Adam banged on the steering wheel. "But what does it mean? It doesn't make any sense."

"Well, we thought they were digging," I said. "And they are. That's something. You didn't see any other clues?"

"To tell you the truth, all those rooms full of dirt more or less knocked anything else out of my mind. I couldn't believe it. It was unreal! I tell you, Mary Ann, these people are more than strange!"

I narrowed my eyes. "You didn't happen to notice if they had raised up any of the floorboards, did you?"

He looked at me. "It did look as if they'd rolled the carpet up in the living room. What are you getting at?"

"Don't you see? They must be digging under the house. That's why we couldn't find any signs of digging in the backyard or down by the dock. They've just lifted the floorboards and started digging under the living room. The loud music they keep playing must be supposed to help cover the sounds of the digging. Where are you driving to?"

"Just around. I don't know about you, but I don't want to go back to the dance." He lifted a hand from the steering wheel and considered it critically. "Look at that," he said, "I'm practically shaking. I don't think I want to make a career of breaking and entering."

"Let's drive out to the beach," I said. "We can talk there."

He gave me an odd look, but obediently turned the car in the direction of the beach. When we got there, we parked and I slipped out of my strappy sandals. We walked out onto the beach.

The moon was floating low over the water and the surf roared like a distant train. With a little stab of surprise I realized that in the past few weeks, I had actually begun to like the beach. I knelt down and began digging in the sand with my fingers.

"Crikey, Mary Ann," said Adam. "Is this any time to be building sand castles? Are you going out of your flipping mind?"

"Look here," I said, burrowing my hand under the sand and firming the sand around it. "Maybe they're not digging a hole," I said. "Maybe they're digging a tunnel. They're tunneling into the castle."

"What castle? Are you feeling all right?"

"Not a *real* castle, dum-dum. The fortress next door—Councilman Fuller's house, with it's super-special burglar alarm."

"Why would they want to be digging into Councilman Fuller's house?" asked Adam.

I stood up, noticing with regret that my filmy dress had gotten some sand and salt water on its hem. "They'd have to have a very very good reason, wouldn't they? I think I know what it could be. Remember when I told you about that creepy little man I saw going around back at Councilman Fuller's house? The one with the suitcase? Well, what if that little man were some go-between and what if Councilman Fuller was some kind of king-pin in the drug racket?"

This time, Adam didn't laugh about the little man I had seen. "You think he has a cache of drugs in the house?" he asked. "That would give them a reason to want to tunnel in, I guess." He looked out to sea at the moon tracing a shining path on the water and suddenly said, "Let's get out of here. I'm getting the creeps."

"It all fits," I said. I carried my sandals as we walked up to the car through the soft sand above the water mark. "Verena told me she had to have jewels and fine cars and that she was too special to get a regular job. Stealing drugs would be just her kind of thing. Good pay. Short hours. And Councilman Fuller won't be reporting the theft to the police, either.''

"If Fuller is in it the way you say," Adam said, "though, he'd kill them if he caught them at it."

"Well, we know they're nervous about getting caught at it, don't we? Look at how they tried to kill you when you started getting nosy."

"That's right," he said, realization dawning. "Those two aren't exactly pussycats themselves. You know, I think you may have something. You think Councilman Fuller is really into all that?"

"Nothing else fits." I smiled to myself. "I remember Verena said she was 'interested in faraway places.' I'll bet they plan to put lots of distance between themselves and Fuller once they get hold of the cache."

"But how did they even know Fuller had the drugs?"

"There's only one way they could know. That guy with the sunglasses must be in the drug trade himself. That's why he didn't want the creepy little man to see him. That's why he's always wearing sunglasses. He's afraid they'll recognize him."

We got in the car and Adam turned on the ignition. "This is serious," he said. "If we're up against what you think, we'd better get word to the cops right away."

I lowered my voice. "What if the cops are involved? Councilman Fuller is very friendly with the police chief."

Adam looked stymied for a moment. Then he said, "I'll call Steve. He'll know what to do."

Chapter Nine

Adam called his brother when we got in Saturday night and tried him again on Sunday morning, both times with no luck. It was obvious the family was away for the weekend. Meanwhile, I was sure Verena and company were burrowing away like moles. They might finish the tunnel any minute, and I knew that once they had what they wanted, they would vanish from the neighborhood like smoke.

I was anxiously peering out the window at their house when Mom came in my room and opened my closet door. "I want to put your dance dress with the things that are supposed to go to the cleaners tomorrow," she said, taking out the dress.

I was staring so intently at the trailer in Verena's driveway that I didn't even turn around. I wondered what was in that trailer. Timber to reinforce the tunnel, maybe?

"Mary Ann! What's happened to your dress?" Mom exclaimed. "It's all stiff along the hem. Something's spilled on it."

I turned around to regard her with anxious eyes. I had forgotten about getting the dress messed up at the beach. "Goodness, I believe that's sand!" she said, flicking some of the caked sand off with her fingers. "What on earth was going on at that dance?"

"Oh," I said sheepishly. "I must have got it a little wet when we went by the beach."

"You went by the beach?"

"We weren't having a very good time at the dance. It was, well... boring. So we left early and went out to the beach."

Mom was looking at me incredulously.

"We built a sand castle," I finished lamely.

Mom sat down on my bed. "Sweetheart, let me get this straight. You and Adam found the dance boring, so you went to the beach in the middle of the night and in your evening dress?"

"It seemed like a good idea at the time. Plenty of fresh air. Uh, no crowds."

"You are seeing too much of Adam," Mom said suddenly. "I've been afraid of that all along."

"I don't see that much of him," I protested.

"You've been seeing him almost every day."

"Oh, well, if you count lunch."

"Let me finish, please, Mary Ann. Darling, can't you see that when you lose interest in seeing your other friends, when you pass up one of the most special dances of the year so that you can go off together and be alone, can't you see that you are *overinvolved*."

Mom had a way of saying "overinvolved" so that it sounded like "leprosy."

"You are far too young to be taking this kind of interest in a boy. Adam's father told your dad that both his other boys married young and maybe that's the kind of thing they do in Adam's family, but it's not what your father and I want for you. We want you to go to college, to have the freedom to develop your interests and make your own circle of friends before you start to take on adult responsibilities."

"But Mom, I am going to go to college! Adam wants to go to college, too. You've got it completely wrong. I'm not overinvolved. I don't think Adam even particularly likes me."

She looked grave. "If Adam doesn't particularly like you, perhaps you'll explain to me why you're going out with him."

"Oh, he likes me, Mom. I just mean he doesn't *like* me."

I was relieved to see a glimmer of humor in her eyes. "I'm not sure I see the distinction you're trying to make."

"I mean we're just friends. Good friends. Nothing lovey-dovey at all."

She got up. "I'm relieved to hear it. Just the same, I want to see you in the weeks to come showing an interest in something else besides Adam Kincaid. Whatever happened to the reading you used to do? The needlepoint? When's the last time you were at church group? Believe me, Mary Ann, I am dead serious about this."

I had the feeling she didn't completely believe that Adam and I had a platonic relationship, but I had bigger problems on my mind just then. After she left, I peeked out the window again. I knew it wouldn't relieve Mom's mind a bit to find out that it was not Adam I was so involved with, but breaking up the neighborhood drug ring.

I was getting in the tub that evening, when I heard the phone ring. I jumped. Lately, everything made me jump. Mom came into the hall. "It's Adam," she said, in a tone heavy with meaning. "I'll tell him you'll call him back."

"No! No!" I said. I quickly wrapped a towel around me and hopped across the hall on one foot while I tried to dry my dripping foot with the trailing end of the towel. "I'll take it in my room."

"Such devoted friendship," I heard Mom mutter as she turned back toward the kitchen.

I was careful to close the door to my bedroom tightly before I picked up the phone. "Hi, Adam," I said breathlessly. "Have you got through to Steve yet?"

"Yeah. Finally. I thought it was better to put it to him as a hypothetical question. You know, 'what would a person do if he had a good reason to think...' et cetera, et cetera."

"So what did he say?"

"It turns out there's a special force that handles this kind of case. You know, where you think there might be local corruption. The FDLE. Stands for Florida Department of Law Enforcement. I got the number of their area office and I already called it, but I didn't get an answer. I guess they close up for the weekend. Heck of a way to fight crime, huh? Closing up for the weekend."

"We'd better call them first thing Monday," I said. "Who knows when Verena and that guy are going to break through into the Fullers' house? They're probably burrowing night and day."

"You sound like a termite ad. I don't think they're making very quick progress. They must have been working on it for weeks now."

"Exactly," I said darkly.

"I'll call the FDLE first thing," he promised.

After school on Monday Adam called to tell me that the FDLE agent was going to come to his house at four and that I should come over there so we could talk to him together.

I knew it would only take me ten minutes to get to Adam's house, but I couldn't wait. At 3:30, I grabbed my car keys and headed out the door.

"So long, Mom. I'm off. I'll be back for supper."

"Where are you going?" She folded her arms.

"Over to Adam's house."

"Are his parents at home?"

"Sure," I gulped. I just had to get to see the FDLE agent. I would die if I missed out on talking to him.

"I thought you told me Adam's mother worked," said Mom, with a look that would have fast frozen a giant mastodon.

"Mom, this is important! I've just *got* to go over there."

"You are not going over to Adam's house when his parents aren't there and that's final," she said, turning back toward the kitchen. "He is welcome to come over here if he'd like to see you."

"What if we just sat out on the front steps at Adam's house and talked?" I wheedled.

"You may invite him over here," she repeated.

I ran back into my room and called Adam. "Adam? This is Mary Ann. Mom won't let me come over to your house because your parents aren't there. Can't we meet anywhere else?''

"How about at Tizzy's? When he gets here, I'll explain things to him and we'll meet you at Tizzy's. He's going to be in plain clothes, so it ought to be okay."

"You are a true friend, Adam," I said fervently. "I'll just die if I miss out on this. I'll see you at Tizzy's."

I found Mom in the kitchen scraping carrots with unusual force. "Be careful," I said when I saw the carrot scrapings flying. "The way you're going you could cut yourself. Look, Mom, I just talked to Adam and we're going to meet at Tizzy's. Okay? You can call up Tizzy's and ask Mr. Jackson if I'm not there if you don't trust me. All right?"

"I do trust you, Mary Ann," she said, giving the carrot a fearful swipe. "I simply have more experience with life than you do and I am making some effort to keep from getting in a situation that you are not ready to handle."

"Right. Fine. All right. Understood. Well, see you at suppertime. Thanks, Mom."

I rushed out of the house before she had time to change her mind. If Sherlock Holmes had had to cope with a mother like mine, I thought, the Hound of the Baskervilles would still be at large.

I hurried, so I got to Tizzy's ages before Adam and the agent. I was forced to eat an entire banana split before they even arrived, which made me feel a little sick. Finally, Adam came in, trailed by a tall, mild-looking man who was wearing gray flannel pants and a white shirt with the sleeves rolled up. I suspected he had ditched his tie and coat at the last minute in an effort to blend in with the dress that was standard at Tizzy's. He and Adam came straight back to the table I had taken near the video machines.

The agent pulled up a chair across from me. I noticed that his hair was beginning to thin. "Adam said you would fill me in on what you two think you're onto," he said quietly.

"You haven't told him about the dirt?" I asked Adam.

"I thought we'd better do it all at once," Adam said. A waitress came by then and Adam and the agent ordered sundaes.

After the sundaes came, I began at the beginning and told him about how Verena had evaded the roadblock. When we told him about what had happened the night Adam painted the water tower, I sensed his interest was picking up.

"You're sure someone was actually shooting at you?" he asked. "It couldn't have been a car backfiring?"

"I've done a lot of hunting," said Adam. "It was a rifle, all right. I heard the shot ricochet off the water tower. That's when I hit the deck and started crawling.''

"You don't have any reason to think it was somebody with a personal grudge against you?''

Adam grinned. "Heck, I'm a junior in high school, not some mafioso chief. If somebody had a grudge against me they'd probably just try to punch me out.''

"Who knew you were going to be at the water tower that night?'' asked the agent.

"The whole school,'' I put in.

"Not really,'' Adam protested.

"Just about,'' I said. "It would have been easy for Verena to know you were going to be at the water tower that night. Everybody was talking about it. But that's not the clincher. Tell him about how we broke into Verena's house, Adam.''

"You don't have to tell me any story about how you broke into the house,'' the agent said hastily. "Just tell me what you 'happened to see' in the house. You might have had any number of legitimate ways of seeing what was in the house.''

"Right,'' said Adam. "Well, as I happened to be in the house one night on my legitimate business, I looked in one of the bedrooms and it was full of dirt.''

"He means soil, earth, the stuff you dig out of the ground,'' I explained.

"Full up to the ceiling,'' Adam said.

The agent raised an eyebrow.

"And that wasn't the only room filled with dirt, either," said Adam. "They were essentially camping out in just two rooms. The rest of the place looked to be filled with dirt."

"Adam saw that the carpet had been rolled up in the living room. I think they've lifted the floorboards and they're digging under the house and tunneling their way into the Fullers' house next door. That's the only way they can get into the place, you see, because it's got a fantastic new alarm system. And this would be the perfect time because the Fullers are in the Keys this month on vacation."

"And don't forget about the weird little man you saw over there," Adam said.

Bit by bit we gave the whole story to the agent. He asked a lot of questions, but in the end he just rocked back in his chair and fingered his jaw while he looked at us.

"Well, what do you think?" I asked. "Hadn't you better go on in there and arrest them?"

He sighed. "It's not that easy," he said. "Suppose I did get a warrant and arrest this Verena person and her dad. The most I could get them for would be wanton destruction of property or something. Maybe digging without a permit. You see, digging a tunnel isn't a felony."

"But they're trying to get at the drugs next door. I'm sure of that," I said.

"To tell you the truth, I think you're probably right. We've heard rumors that somebody in the city government here was running drugs. But rumors aren't evidence. There's no way I could get a search warrant for that house with just the evidence you've given me today."

"You mean there's nothing we can do? You mean, they're going to get away with it?"

"I don't know," he said, looking at us seriously. "We might be able to lay some kind of trap. But I'd need your help."

"We'd love to help, wouldn't we, Adam?"

"I'd have to get your parents' permission," he said. "You'd have to tell them the whole story."

A silence fell over the table.

"The whole story?" I said in a small voice. I imagined telling my parents that I had sneaked out of the house in the wee hours of the morning and had ended up in duel with an armed man. I imagined telling them that I had helped Adam break into a neighbor's house. The whole idea gave me a very sick feeling in the pit of my stomach that had nothing to do with the big banana split I had eaten. "I'd get grounded for the rest of my entire life," I said.

"Maybe you wouldn't have to go into all the details. Maybe you could just give them the general drift," Adam said. "What kind of 'help' do you have in mind, sir?"

The agent began fingering his jaw again. "Suppose this Councilman Fuller heard what his neighbors were up to? Isn't there a chance he would rush home and try to spirit away his cache of drugs? If we could catch him red-handed like that, with his arms full of cocaine, we wouldn't need a warrant."

"But how would he find out?" Adam asked.

"That's where Mary Ann comes in," said the agent. "She could call up Fuller and tell him she's noticed something fishy about the neighbors and that her parents don't believe her but she thinks they're trying to get into his house. That ought to set him thinking. It would more or less have to be you, Mary Ann. If your parents thought somebody was breaking into Fullers' house they'd just call the police and ask them to keep an eye on things. You, on the other hand, can play the part of the naive teenager who isn't sure what to do."

I brightened. "That sounds simple. Why can't I just call him up? Why do we have to tell my parents anything?"

"They'd have to agree to let you do it. The thing is, it could be dangerous. These guys are ruthless, believe me. Remember Judge Ritter over on the west coast who was handing down such stiff drug sentences? A few weeks ago, he and his wife went out on their boat and they haven't been heard from since.''

"Maybe this isn't such a good idea," Adam said. "I don't think Mary Ann ought to get involved."

"I won't let Councilman Fuller know that I suspect *him* of anything," I argued. "When I talk to him I'll just act kind of silly and confused. I don't see that they'd have any reason to try to kill me."

"These are violent people," said the agent.

"You don't have to tell us," said Adam. "They've already shot at me, remember? Heck, I don't know, I think we've done our part. It's up to you now. I think Mary Ann ought to stay out of it."

I gulped. "I'll talk to my parents about it," I said.

The agent smiled.

As we were walking out to our cars, Adam said, "I think you're making a mistake."

"I won't have to tell them everything," I said. "I don't have to tell them I was there that night at the water tower. I'll just tell them about you getting shot at. And I don't have to mention that we broke into the house. I can just say that you 'found out' about the dirt. It's all a matter of how I tell the story."

"If you leave out the things your parents aren't going to want to hear, there's not going to be much of a story left," said Adam.

"Get in the car," I said suddenly. "There's Verena."

The agent smoothly slid into his car and Adam got in beside him.

I leaned over and spoke through the open car window. "It was really nice to meet your Uncle Howard," I said in a loud voice. "We'll have to get together again before he goes home. I'll call you."

Verena threw me a curious glance as I was getting into my car. I smiled insincerely in her direction, hoping it wasn't written all over my face that I had just been turning her in to the cops.

Chapter Ten

I have the feeling that you are not telling us the whole story," Mom said.

"I'm giving you all the essential facts." Guilty feelings trickled from my ears down to my sneakers. "You see, Adam and I were sort of working on this case together and he *did* do some of the detective work. So I might not be aware of every *single* detail of the story, but I've given you the main idea. The important thing is, this FDLE agent thinks we might really be onto something."

"I don't know," said Mom. "George Fuller a drug dealer? It seems very strange. A respectable member of the community? Somebody we've known for fifteen years?''

"Well, I have heard people say that George's ethics stink," Dad said slowly. "And it's true that in the past few years he's seemed to have an awful lot of money. The Mercedes, the new boat, the fancy burglar-alarm system. And then there's the way they're always taking vacations. Remember that vacation in Bermuda only a few months ago? How can the man be making so much money when he's always on vacation?''

"It's just hard for me to believe," said Mom. "Poor Louella.''

"Maybe she's in on it," I said darkly.

"Mary Ann! What an idea!" Mom exclaimed.

"Well, whatever is or is not going on, I don't think Mary Ann should get involved," Dad said.

"But I'm already involved!" I protested. "They've already shot at Adam, and they must figure that he's told me whatever he's found out. I could be the next target. The safest thing to do, really, is for me to help the police get all these people locked up.''

Mom looked at Dad. "She has a point, Charles. Besides, at a time like this, I think we do well to remember Kant's categorical imperative.''

I did my best to remember Kant's categorical imperative, but somehow it wouldn't come into focus.

"Suppose everyone refused to help the law enforcement people," Mom went on. "Where would we be then? We have a certain duty."

"Before we decide anything, I want to talk to this agent," said Dad grimly.

The agent must have put a good case to Dad because the next evening, I found myself dialing the number of the Seabreeze Hotel in Key West while Mom, Dad and the FDLE agent sat around me in a circle, being very very quiet.

At last I got put through to the Fullers' room. "Councilman Fuller?" I asked. "Hi. This is Mary Ann Taylor. I live across the street from you... Yes, little Mary Ann. Listen, the reason I called is that I think something really strange is going on at that house next door to you. Mom and Dad think I'm all wrong, but I tell you, I'm sure they're digging over there.... Yes, I said digging...those people from Miami who rented the Peebleses' house. You must have seen them over there before you went on vacation—the guy is always wearing sunglasses... Yes, well it looks to me like they've lifted up the floorboards of the Peebleses' living room and I feel like I've heard sounds of digging.

"I was just reading this mystery book called *The Case of the Secret Tunnel* last night and it suddenly hit me that maybe they were trying to tunnel under the ground to get into your house.... I don't know what made me think that, but it just suddenly came to me and then I remembered how you used to have this coin collection and I just thought I'd feel a lot better if I called you up and told you about it.... Oh, well, I'm really glad to know you sold it. Now I can sleep a lot better. I guess it's stupid but it was really bothering me.... I'd appreciate it if you didn't mention this to my parents, you know? They told me it was really silly.... Maybe you're right. Maybe I have been reading too many mystery books. I hope I haven't bothered you... Are you having a nice vacation...? Good. Well, bye now."

I hung up and looked over at the three anxious faces gathered around me. "He didn't seem very worried," I said. "He kept acting as though it were all my imagination. Do you think I should have said more to convince him? Given some more details?"

"Maybe we're just on the wrong track," said Dad. "Maybe George Fuller's not involved after all."

The agent glanced at his watch and got up. "We've got the house staked out," he said. "Now all we can do is wait."

After the agent left, to my disgust Mom and Dad wouldn't even let me look out the window to see what was going on. "Flying bullets," said Dad tersely.

"I don't see why you're so nervous," I said. "Councilman Fuller can't possibly be back from Key West yet. I was just talking to him."

"If he really is a drug dealer, you don't think he'll come fetch the stuff himself, do you?" said Dad grimly. "He'll probably send somebody else to do it. Some trigger-happy underling, no doubt. They might have machine guns, grenades, cannons. Who knows? I'd drive us all to a motel this minute if I weren't afraid we'd walk outside into a hail of cross fire."

"Can't I just go outside and take a peek to see if I can see the stakeouts?" I pleaded.

"No," said Dad. "You cannot."

Then he made us go sit in the kitchen because it was the room that had the fewest windows and it didn't face the street.

Outside, the neighborhood was crawling with police, a trap was being set for a big drug operation and all because of me, me, me and Adam and our fine detective work. And I had to miss it all. I sat at the kitchen table doing my homework while Dad went around tapping on walls and saying that he wished we'd gone in for a concrete block house instead of a cedar one on account of concrete block being more bulletproof.

"Well, dear," said Mom placidly, "I doubt if the problem will arise again."

"You can sleep in Phil's room, Mary Ann," Dad said, ignoring her. "It faces the back. Or maybe we should lay out a sleeping bag in the hall. The hall is a more protected location. No windows at all."

Luckily, before the time came for me to make my way through the airplane models, the shells and the birds'-egg collections in Phil's room in search of the bed, the phone rang.

Dad snatched it up immediately. "Hello?" he said. He covered the receiver with his hand and whispered, "They've picked up somebody who was trying to take the cocaine out of the Fullers' house."

"What about Verena?" I asked, but Dad didn't seem to hear me. He was too busy listening on the telephone. It seemed he was listening a long time.

"Well, thanks for letting us know," he said finally. "That's really good news."

After he hung up, Mom and I looked at him expectantly. "We can all go to bed now," he announced. "They've arrested half the neighborhood. There's nobody left to do any shooting—" he looked at me wryly "—unless you suspect Mr. Stuart, the truant officer, too."

I followed him while he went around the living room opening the windows. "You mean they've arrested Verena?" I asked.

"Taken her into custody," he corrected, drawing the curtains. "It turns out she was a runaway.

They found that out when they ran her description through their computer today."

"Oh, I can't stand it that we missed all the excitement," I cried. "I didn't even hear the police banging on the door. I didn't even see any flashing blue lights. I didn't even get to see a single one of the stakeouts!"

"In that event, your life must be unbearably dull," said Dad dryly.

"What about that guy in the sunglasses?" I asked. "Did they arrest him, too?"

"Contributing to the delinquency of a minor, I believe," said Dad. "Other charges are expected to follow. He's being fingerprinted."

"Ooo, the thrill of it!" I sighed. "Adam and I did it. We did it! We're crime busters!"

"It's a satisfaction to know that we've done our civic duty," Mom said. She sat down in the rocking chair and opened a book. I noticed it was called *The Critique of Pure Reason*. Mom's idea of a thrill was substantially different from mine.

The phone rang again. "It's probably Adam," I said. "I'll pick it up in my room." I was glad to see that Mom did not grimace at the sound of Adam's name. She had been cheered up by the news that he and I had been spending a lot of our time together doing detection work and I saw signs that her attitude toward him was mellowing.

"Hello?"

"Mary Ann? Adam."

"I thought it might be you. They've actually arrested them! Exciting, huh? What did your parents say when you told them everything?"

"I didn't exactly tell them everything. I sort of skated over that part about breaking into Verena's house. I just let them think I saw inside the house when I gave the wallet back to her and they didn't ask a lot of questions. They were totally floored by the idea of all that dirt heaped up in the Peebleses' house. My dad said he hoped the Peebleses had the 'all perils' type homeowners' coverage."

"What about the water tower? Did you skate over that, too?"

"I didn't have to," Adam said sheepishly. "Yesterday my dad drove by the water tower and he guessed right away who had done it."

"Was he mad?"

"Well, I tried to put it to him that it was a family tradition."

"How did that go down?"

"Not too hot, but at least they haven't started talking about military schools again. Mom did say she wasn't sure that you were quite the right girl to settle me down."

My heart gave a little lurch. I had forgotten all about the arrangement Adam and I had. Now that we had finished our investigation and now that his parents weren't talking about military schools anymore, I guessed we wouldn't be seeing so much of each other.

"I gotta go," Adam said. "On top of everything else, we just got this call that my Aunt Sue has been in a car wreck and we've got to drive up to Jacksonville and see her. I don't know exactly when we'll be getting back. I wanted to stay here while they went without me but they wouldn't let me."

"Wonder why?" I asked lightly.

I could hear the smile in his voice when he said, "Yeah. Well, let's get together as soon as I get back. We've got a lot to talk about."

Like about me giving your ring back, I thought. I swallowed. "Sure," I said. "Call me."

The next day, it was nice not having to look at Verena preening herself in the cafeteria, but it was lonely not having Adam around. I realized that I was going to miss him a lot when he slipped back into his usual world of blondes in bikinis, of frogging and fishing.

Adam and his family were gone the next couple of days, but when I got in from school on Friday, there was a note taped to my front door. "We're back," it said. "Can you meet me at Tizzy's at four? Adam."

When I went in, Mom was in the kitchen putting away groceries. "Did you see Adam when he came by?" I asked her.

"No, darling. I've been out shopping."

"Well, he left a note. I'm going to meet him at Tizzy's at four."

"That's good," she said, putting a can of soup on the shelf. "Did you see that the whole story broke in the paper today? They arrested George Fuller at his hotel in Key West. Poor Louella. What a terrible shock for her. You ought to take the paper with you to show Adam. If he's been out of town while all this was breaking, you two will have a lot to talk about."

"Yes," I said, bleakly, "we will."

That afternoon when I walked in Tizzy's front door, Adam was already at our usual table back by the video games. He grinned and waved. I felt a little lump in my throat thinking of the first time I had seen him sitting there the day I came in to satisfy my curiosity. I made my way back to our table and handed him the newspaper.

"Oh, great!" he said. "I missed seeing this." He spread it out on the table. Verena had made the front page. "Tears of Joy," read the caption. "Kidnapped Teen Reunited with Family at Last."

"Kidnapped!" he whooped.

I smiled a little. "Nice touch, huh?"

He read aloud, "'I was afraid for my life,' the teenager told the *Herald* in her modest South Hialeah home. 'I knew he was violent. He had threatened me many times with a gun. I was watched constantly. I was terrified, too afraid to call my parents. I didn't know what to do.'" Adam looked up at me. "What a nerve!" he exclaimed. "I guess we're supposed to believe he forced her to take that Corvette from him and that little wallet with the rubies on it. Do you think she can get away with this junk?"

"Maybe so," I said. "You didn't think she was up to anything at first."

"Unbe*lievable*," said Adam. "Hey, I see here they got one and a half million dollars' worth of cocaine from Fuller's house. That creepy little guy of yours walked right into their arms carrying it."

"You'll notice, it was in a suitcase."

"I'll never be able to look at a suitcase again without a shiver, I promise you," he said, folding up the paper.

"Hi, Adam! Hi, Mary Ann!" called Amy. She and Larry took the table nearest ours and Amy leaned over in our direction to say confidentially, "Isn't it incredible about Verena? Who'd have suspected it? I never dreamed she'd been kidnapped."

Adam snorted.

"It just goes to show you can't be too careful," Larry said in his froglike voice. "It's a scary world out there."

"Let's get out of here," Adam muttered to me.

"But we just got here!" I said, bewildered.

"Let's go," he said, getting up.

"Where are we going?" I asked.

"I don't know. Out."

A few moments later we were driving across the bridge toward the beach. "Your friend Amy is the worst," he said. "Always nosing around."

"I think she just wanted to talk about the drug bust," I said. November weather had come on us suddenly. The skies had gone gray and blowy and there was a nip in the air. "Nobody's going to be at the beach on a day like this," I said.

"That's what I'm hoping," he said grimly.

When he threw the car door open, I got out. The wind whipped some sand into my face and I blinked rapidly. We took off our shoes and walked out toward the ocean. There were flecks of white foam far out and the waves were dark and gray.

Adam picked up a broken shell and tossed it ahead of us. As it hit the hard sand, some plovers took flight and quickly disappeared into the grayness ahead of us.

"I don't know why anybody would want to be inside when they can be outside," he said, looking at the sky.

Feeling the grit whipped against my skin, I could think of a few reasons, but I said meekly, "I don't either."

"You remember when I gave you my ring?" he asked suddenly.

"Yes," I said. There was a lump in my throat but if Adam had dragged me out to the beach because he was afraid I would make a scene in Tizzy's when he wanted his ring back, he would find out that I wasn't that kind of person. "I haven't lost it either. Here it is." I slipped the chain over my head and held it out to him.

"You want to give it back to me?" he said blankly.

"Sure," I said, feeling a little confused.

"Well, if you *want* to give it back to me," he said. He kicked a little sand with his heel as we walked.

"I want to give it back to you if you're ready to have it back," I said, running a little to catch up with him.

He turned and looked at me. I was reminded once again of the Wanted bills put up in the post office. There was a decided resemblance, there, yes, when he lowered those black eyebrows of his.

"Look, this is getting confusing," he said. "Why don't you just tell me straight? Do you think it makes sense for you and me to go out together?"

"What?"

"I mean, for real. Like guys and girls do. Do you follow me?"

"I think so." I looked at him hesitantly. "Do we?" I asked.

"Good grief, Mary Ann. Don't go sticking your neck out or anything," he said ironically.

I thought fast. "Yes," I said.

He grinned. "Good," he said. He thrust a hand into his pocket. "I got something for you."

The sand that was being whipped into my eyes had filled my eyes with tears but I could make out that he was holding out something gold and glittery. I took it from him and turned my back to the wind to look at it. It was a plain gold heart hanging on a chain and something was written on it. I wiped the tears and sand out of my eye with shirtsleeve and peered at it.

In delicate italic script was written, *For my favorite accomplice.*

"Oh, Adam!" I said, tears filling my eyes again. "It's so sweet."

"It wasn't cheap, but, what the hey, you saved my life that night at the water tower." He grinned. "Now we're even."

He bent over and kissed me. With the cold wind throwing sand against our faces and the sea spray dampening our shirts, we clung together for a minute, feeling the warmness of being so close. The roaring ocean was ambitiously working itself up past small craft warnings. A cold wave, more venturesome than the rest, licked at my bare heel and I could feel an insane grin growing on my face. Going with Adam was short on moonlight and roses, but it had its compensations.

WATCH FOR THESE TITLES FROM FIRST LOVE COMING NEXT MONTH

FUTURE TENSE
Joan Hess
Was Moran reading Carter's lips, or his mind? Both were of interest to her.

TREASURE OF THE HILLS
Mary Virginia Fox
Peter's first love had always been the sea, but now it looked as though he would never see it again. Was this the end of his dream, or the beginning of a new one?

NIGHTS ON THE BAYOU
Miriam Morton
Now that Shelby had met Jon she understood much more about her own Cajun heritage, but would he also be able to clarify her future?

KING FOR QUEEN
Judy Mayer
Though Karen King had been nominated homecoming queen, she hated the idea. How could she make sure that she wouldn't get elected?

First Love from Silhouette